DALMATIAN PRESS

American
CLASSICS
FOR CHILDREN
COLLECTION I

American
CLASSICS
FOR CHILDREN
COLLECTION I

The Adventures of
Tom Sawyer

MARK TWAIN

※

The Adventures of
Huckleberry Finn

MARK TWAIN

※

Moby Dick

HERMAN MELVILLE

Dalmatian 🐾 Press

The Dalmatian Press American Classics for Children
have been adapted and illustrated with care and thought,
to introduce you to a world of famous authors, characters, ideas,
and great stories that have been loved for generations.

Editor — Kathryn Knight
Creative Director — Gina Rhodes
And the entire classics project team of Dalmatian Press

ALL ART AND ADAPTED TEXT © DALMATIAN PRESS, LLC

ISBN: 1-40370-471-6

First Published in the United States in 2003 by Dalmatian Press, LLC, USA

Copyright © 2003 Dalmatian Press, LLC

Printed and bound in the U.S.A.

The DALMATIAN PRESS name and logo are
trademarks of Dalmatian Press, LLC, Franklin, Tennessee 37067.

12597

03 04 05 06 07 LBM 15 14 13 12 11 10 9 8 7 6 5 4 3 2 1

FOREWORD

A note to the reader—

Three American classic stories rest in your hands. The characters are famous. The tales are timeless.

Each story has been carefully condensed and adapted from the original version (which you really *must* read when you're ready for every detail). We kept the well-known phrases for you. We kept the author's style. And we kept the important imagery and heart of each tale.

Literature is terrific fun! It encourages you to think. It helps you dream. It is full of heroes and villains, suspense and humor, adventure and wonder, and new ideas. It introduces you to writers who reach out across time to say: "Do you want to hear a story I wrote?"

Curl up and enjoy.

DALMATIAN PRESS
AMERICAN CLASSICS FOR CHILDREN

COLLECTION I

The Adventures of Tom Sawyer
The Adventures of Huckleberry Finn
Moby Dick

❦

COLLECTION II

Little Women
Pollyanna
Rebecca of Sunnybrook Farm

CONTENTS

The Adventures of Tom Sawyer

MARK TWAIN

CONDENSED AND ADAPTED BY
W.T. ROBINSON

ILLUSTRATED BY
RUTH PALMER

CONTENTS

TOM SAWYER — a kid full of spunk and mischief who is *not* the model boy of St. Petersburg, Missouri

AUNT POLLY — Tom's Aunt who took him in when his parents died

SID SAWYER — Tom's younger half-brother

COUSIN MARY — Tom's older cousin, Aunt Polly's daughter

HUCKLEBERRY FINN — the young outcast of the village who lives on his own

BECKY THATCHER — the lovely new girl in town who steals Tom's heart

MR. DOBBINS — the strict schoolmaster

Tom's buddies
JEFF THATCHER — Becky's cousin
JIM — the little boy who helps Aunt Polly
BEN ROGERS — the "*Big Missouri* steamboat"
JOE HARPER — a fellow pirate

INJUN JOE — a mean, lying villain with revenge on his mind

MUFF POTTER — a foolish ol' man who gets mixed up with Injun Joe

DOCTOR ROBINSON — a young (unfortunate) doctor in town

The pirates of Jackson's Island
THE BLACK AVENGER OF THE SPANISH MAIN
HUCK FINN THE RED-HANDED
THE TERROR OF THE SEAS

THE "SPANIARD" — a mysterious stranger in town… in disguise

THE RAGGED MAN — the Spaniard's partner

THE WELSHMAN, MR. JONES — the old man who lives on Cardiff Hill

JUDGE THATCHER — Becky's father

WIDOW DOUGLAS — the rich old lady whose life is saved by Huck Finn

The Adventures of
Tom Sawyer

CHAPTER ONE

Y-o-u-u, Tom – The Thread of a Tale

"Tom!"

No answer.

"*Tom!*"

No answer.

"What's going on with that boy, I wonder? You, TOM!"

No answer.

"Well, I declare, if I get hold of you I'll—"

The old lady did not finish, for by this time she was bending down and punching under the bed with the broom. She found nothing but the cat. She went to the open door and looked out among the tomato vines and weeds in the garden. No Tom.

"Y-o-u-u, *Tom*!"

There was a slight noise behind her, and she turned just in time to catch a small boy by the back of his jacket and stop his escape.

"There! I might-a thought of that closet. What you been doing in there?"

"Nothing."

"Nothing! Look at your hands. And look at your mouth. What *is* that mess?"

"I don't know, Aunt."

"Well, *I* know. It's jam—that's what it is. Forty times I've said if you didn't let that jam alone I'd wallop you. Hand me that switch."

The switch hung in the air.

"My! Look behind you, Aunt!"

The old lady whirled round and snatched her skirts out of danger. The boy ran in an instant, scrambled up the high board fence, and disappeared over it.

His Aunt Polly stood surprised a moment and then broke into a gentle laugh.

"Hang the boy, can't I never learn anything? Ain't he played enough tricks on me like that by now? He's full of the Old Devil, but he's my own dead sister's boy, poor thing, and I ain't got the heart

to whip him, somehow. I know he'll skip school this afternoon, so I'll just have to make him work tomorrow to punish him. He hates to work on Saturdays more than he hates anything else, and I've *got* to do something or I'll spoil the child."

Tom *did* skip school, and he had a very good time. He got home just in time to help Jim, Auntie's little helper, saw and split the next-day's wood before supper. Tom's younger half-brother, Sid, was already through with his part of the work. (Sid was a quiet boy who never got in much trouble.)

That evening, Tom sat for supper with Sid, Cousin Mary, and Aunt Polly. While Tom was eating, Aunt Polly asked him sly and clever questions—trying to find out if he had skipped out of school that afternoon to go swimming.

"Tom, it was kinda warm in school, warn't it?"

"Yes'm."

"Real warm, warn't it?"

"Yes'm."

"Didn't you want to go swimming, Tom?"

A bit of a scare shot through Tom.

"No'm—well, not very much."

The old lady reached out and felt Tom's shirt. "But you ain't too warm now, though, are you?"

Tom could see what she was up to.

"Some of us pumped water on our heads," he said, "and mine's still wet. See?"

Aunt Polly was upset to think Tom might be fooling her. Then she thought of something…

"Tom, surely you didn't have to undo your shirt collar where I sewed it together, just to pump water on your head, did you?"

Tom felt better. He opened his jacket. His shirt collar was still tightly sewed.

"Bother! Well, go 'long with you," said Aunt Polly. "I thought sure you'd skipped school and been swimming. But I forgive you, Tom. *This* time."

She was half sorry her trick had failed, and half glad that Tom had done the right thing for once.

But Sid said, "Well, now, I thought you sewed his collar with *white* thread, but now it's sewed with *black* thread."

"Why, I did sew it with white! Tom!"

"Siddy, I'll get you for that," shouted Tom, running out the door.

After Tom had scrambled over the back fence, he found a safe place to hide and plan his revenge on Sid. He also had to figure out just how he had messed up on re-sewing his collar.

He looked at the two large needles stuck under the collar of his jacket. One needle had white thread and the other black. Tom wished Aunt Polly would stick to one color or the other. "I can't keep up with 'em," he thought.

He got home pretty late that night. His clothes were dirty and torn from scuffling on the ground. Aunt Polly caught him climbing in his window and knew just the kind of Saturday work she would give him.

CHAPTER TWO

Whitewashing – The New Girl

Saturday morning came. Every child was happy to be out of school for the day—all except Tom.

He appeared on the sidewalk with a bucket of white paint and a long-handled brush. He looked at the fence—thirty yards of high, board fence. He sat down on a tree-box, sad and unhappy.

Jim came skipping along with a tin pail, singing. Bringing water from the town pump had always been hateful work for Tom, but now it did not seem so. He remembered that there were always children at the pump, joking around and trading playthings.

Tom said, "Say, Jim, I'll go get the water if you'll whitewash some."

Jim shook his head. "Can't, Tom. Your Aunt Polly, she tole me I got to go an' git dis water. She say she spec' you would ask me to whitewash, an' so she tole me go 'long an' not to help you—she say *she'd* be boss of de whitewashin'."

"Oh, never you mind what she said, Jim. That's the way she always talks. Gimme the bucket—I won't be gone only a minute. *She* won't ever know."

"Oh, I can't. Ole Miss Polly, she'd whup me good. 'Deed she would."

"*She!* She never spanks anybody hard. She talks awful, but talk don't hurt you much. Jim, I'll give you the most special marble. I'll give you a white alley! It's the finest shootin' marble there is!"

"My! Dat's a mighty fine marble, I tell you! But I'se powerful 'fraid of Miss Polly—"

"And besides, if you'll paint, I'll show you my swollen sore toe. I'll take off the bandage. "

Jim couldn't say no to *this*. He put down his pail, took the marble, and bent over the toe. In another moment he was flying down the street with his pail and a stinging bottom, Tom was busy whitewashing, and Aunt Polly was leaving with a slipper in her hand and victory in her eye.

Tom tried to think of a way out of the mess he was in. Then he got a great idea.

He picked up his brush and went to work. Ben Rogers came in sight, hop-skip-and-jumping, happy as could be. He was eating an apple and giving a long whoo-oop at times, followed by a deep ding-dong-dong, ding-dong-dong—pretending to be the *Big Missouri* river steamboat. He was the boat, captain and engine-bells all at the same time.

"Stop her, sir! Ting-a-ling-ling! Ting-a-ling-ling! Chow! Ch-ch-chow! Chow! Done with the engines, sir! Ting-a-ling-ling! *Shsst, Shsst, Shsst!*" (letting off some steam pressure).

Tom went on whitewashing, paying no attention to Ben, the steamboat. Ben stared a moment and said, "Hi-yi! *You're* in a mess, ain't you!"

No answer. Tom looked at his last paint stroke with the eye of an artist. Tom's mouth watered for the apple, but he stuck to his work.

Ben said, "Hello, old chap, you gotta work, hey?"

Tom turned suddenly.

"Why, it's you, Ben! I hadn't noticed you."

"Say—I'm going in a-swimming, I am. Don't you wish you could? But of course you'd rather *work*—wouldn't you? Course you would!"

Tom studied the boy a bit, and said:

"What do you call work?"

"Why, ain't *that* work?"

"Well, maybe it is, and maybe it ain't. All I know is—it's fun for Tom Sawyer."

"Oh, come, now, you don't mean to say you *like* it?"

The paintbrush kept moving.

"Like it? Well, I don't see why I shouldn't like it. Does a boy get a chance to whitewash a fence every day?"

That changed the way Ben thought about it. He stopped nibbling his apple and began watching Tom closely, getting more and more interested. Soon he said:

"Say, Tom, let *me* whitewash a little."

Tom thought about it and was about to agree, but he changed his mind.

"No—no—I reckon I better not, Ben. You see, Aunt Polly wants this fence done right. I reckon there ain't one boy in a thousand, maybe two thousand, that can do it the way it's got to be done."

"No—is that so? Oh, come, now—lemme just try. Only just a little—I'd let *you*, if you was me, Tom."

"Ben, I'd like to, honest injun, but Aunt Polly—
well, Jim wanted to do it, but she wouldn't let him.
Won't let Sid, neither. Now don't you see my
problem? If you was to try this fence and anything
was to happen to it—"

"Oh, shucks, I'll be just as careful. Now lemme
try. Say—I'll give you the core of my apple."

"Well, here… No, Ben, I can't. I'm afraid—"

"I'll give you *all* of it!"

Tom gave up the brush, acting like he didn't want to stop painting, but knowing that his plan had worked just right. And while Ben worked and sweated in the sun, Tom sat on a barrel in the shade close by, munched his apple, and planned how he could trap some more kids. He didn't have to wait long. Boys stopped by every little while. They came to laugh at Tom, but stayed to paint the fence.

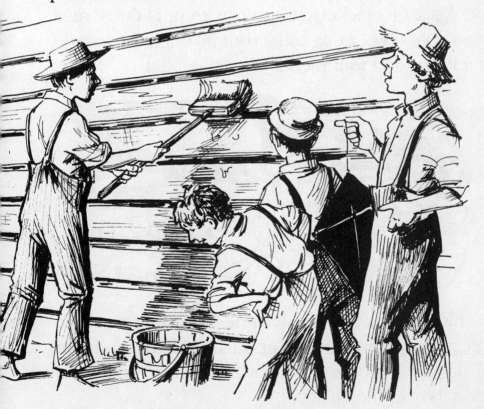

By the time Ben was tired out, Tom had traded the next chance to Billy Fisher for a kite. When he gave up, Johnny Miller traded for a dead rat and a string to swing it with—and so it went, hour after hour. And when the middle of the afternoon came, Tom was rich, for he also had twelve marbles, part of a harmonica, a piece of blue bottle-glass to look through, a piece of red chalk, a key that wouldn't unlock anything, a tin soldier, a couple of tadpoles, a spool, six firecrackers, a kitten with only one eye, a brass doorknob, a dog collar (but no dog), the handle of a knife, and four pieces of orange peel.

He had fun the whole time, and the fence had three coats of whitewash on it! If he hadn't run out of paint he would have emptied the pockets of every boy in the village.

Tom had figured out that in order to make a man or a boy want something, all you had to do was make the thing hard to get. He thought about his good luck and went back inside the house.

Tom reported to Aunt Polly. "May I go and play now, Aunt?"

"What, already? How much have you done?"

"It's all done, Aunt."

"Tom, don't lie to me."

"I ain't, Aunt. It *is* all done."

Aunt Polly didn't trust Tom. She went out to see for herself. When she found the whole fence whitewashed with three coats, she could hardly believe her eyes.

"Well, there's no getting round it, you can work when you want to, Tom. Go 'long and play, but get back soon, or I'll spank you."

She was so happy with what he had done that she gave him a big red apple and read him a Bible verse about how good it was to work hard for special treats. While her back was turned, Tom snitched a doughnut.

Then Tom skipped out and saw Sid. Soon the air was full of mud balls falling on Sid like a hailstorm, and before Aunt Polly could catch him, Tom was over the fence and gone. He was happy now that he had gotten even with Sid for getting him in trouble over his black thread.

Tom hurried toward town, where the boys were setting up two armies for a battle. Tom was General of one of these armies, Joe Harper was General of the other. Tom's army won a great victory. When the "dead" were counted and all prisoners returned, Tom turned toward home.

As Tom was passing by the house where Jeff Thatcher lived, he saw a girl in the garden—a lovely little blue-eyed girl with long, yellow braids. The great war hero fell without firing a shot. Who was this new girl? In less than a second he forgot Amy Lawrence, his girlfriend of the past week.

He stared at this new angel secretly, till he was sure she had seen him. Then he pretended he did not know she was there, and began to show off.

While he was in the middle of some cartwheels, he glanced up and saw that the little girl was headed toward the house. Tom came up to the fence, hoping she would stay awhile longer. She stopped a moment on the steps and tossed a pansy over the fence as she went out of sight.

Tom was thrilled!

He slipped over to the flower and picked it up between his bare toes so nobody would notice. Then, hopping off a short distance, he put the pansy inside his jacket. He hung around the fence till sunset, "showing off" as before, and hoping that she was watching him through a window. Finally he went home, with his poor head in a whirl.

All through supper Tom seemed so happy that his aunt wondered what was going on. He took a good scolding for mud-balling Sid, and didn't even seem to care.

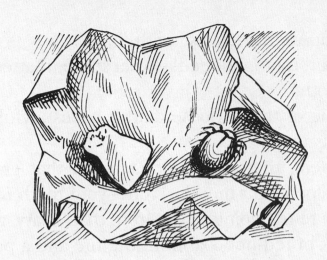

CHAPTER THREE

Huck Finn – Becky Thatcher

Monday morning came. Tom Sawyer was unhappy. Mondays always made him that way—because it began another week's slow suffering in school.

Tom lay thinking. Maybe he could be sick and stay home from school. What could he think of? Suddenly he had an idea. One of his upper front teeth was loose. This was lucky. He began groaning.

Before long, Sid, Cousin Mary, and Aunt Polly were there to see what the trouble was.

"You, Tom! Tom, what's the matter with you?"

"Oh, Auntie, I'm—"

"What's the matter with you, child?"

"Oh, Auntie, it's my tooth!"

"Your tooth, indeed! What's the matter with your tooth?"

"One of them's loose, and it aches awful—just perfectly awful."

"There, there, now, don't begin that groaning again. Open your mouth. Well—your tooth *is* loose, but you're not going to die from that. Mary, get me a chunk of red-hot coal from the fire and a piece of silk thread."

"Oh, please, Auntie, please don't pull it out. It don't hurt any more. I don't want to stay home from school."

"Oh, you don't, don't you? So all this fuss was because you thought you'd get to stay home from school and go a-fishing? Tom, Tom, I love you so, but you seem to try every way you can to break my old heart."

By this time the dental tools were ready. Aunt Polly tied one end of the silk thread round Tom's tooth and tied the other to the bedpost. Then she seized the chunk of fire and suddenly thrust it almost into the boy's face. The tooth was now dangling by the bedpost.

So Tom didn't get out of going to school, but he was able to spit in a new way through the new gap in his teeth. Lots of boys crowded around him on his way to school to get a look at his terrific spitting tricks. Tom thought that even having a tooth pulled could turn out to be a good thing.

Shortly, Tom came upon the young outcast of the village, Huckleberry Finn. Huckleberry had no mother to care for him and was always getting into trouble. All the mothers of St. Petersburg disliked him, but Tom and the other boys wished they had his freedom. Aunt Polly had ordered Tom not to play with Huckleberry, so of course he played with him every chance he got. Huckleberry was always dressed in his Pa's hand-me-down rags. His hat was a mess and his coat hung nearly to the ground. One suspender held up his baggy trousers.

Huckleberry came and went as he pleased. He slept on doorsteps in good weather and in empty barrels in wet. He did not have to go to school or church. He stayed up late. He went fishing or swimming whenever he wanted, and he was always the first boy to go barefoot in the spring. He never had to wash or put on clean clothes. Every boy in St. Petersburg thought he had a perfect life.

"Hello, Huckleberry!" said Tom.

"Hello yourself, and see how you like it."

"What's that you got?"

"Dead cat."

"Lemme see him, Huck. My, he's pretty stiff. Where'd you get him?"

"Bought him off'n a boy."

"What did you give for it?"

"I give a blue marble that I bought off Ben Rogers for a hoop-stick."

"Say—what is dead cats good for, Huck?"

"Good to get rid of warts."

"How do you do that?"

"Why, you take your cat and go and get in the graveyard around midnight when somebody that was wicked has been buried. When it's midnight, devils will come makin' devil's-fire an' all. When they're taking that dead feller away, you toss your cat after 'em and say, 'Devil follow dead man, cat follow devil, warts follow cat, *I'm* done with you!' That'll get rid of *any* wart."

"Sounds right. Say, Hucky, when you going to try the cat?"

"Tonight. I reckon the devils'll come after old Hoss Williams' body tonight."

"Will ya lemme go with you?"

"Sure—if you ain't scared."

"Scared! 'Tain't likely. Will you *me-yow* like a cat outside my window when you come to get me?"

"Yes—and you me-yow back. Last time, you kep' me a-me-yowing forever."

"I couldn't me-yow that night becuz Auntie was watching me, but I'll me-yow this time, honest. Say—what ya got there?"

"Nothing but a tick bug."

"Where'd you get him?"

"Out in the woods."

"What'll you take for him?"

"I don't know. I don't want to sell him."

"Say, Huck—I'll give you my tooth for him."

"Less see it."

Tom got out a bit of paper and unrolled it.

"Is it real?"

Tom showed him the hole between his teeth.

"Well, all right," said Huckleberry, "it's a trade."

The boys went their own ways, each feeling richer than before.

When Tom reached the little schoolhouse, he walked in quickly as if he had been trying to hurry as fast as he could. The schoolmaster spotted him.

"Thomas Sawyer!"

Tom knew he was in trouble when he heard his full name used.

"Sir!"

"Come up here," said the schoolmaster. "Now, sir, why are you late again, as usual?"

Tom was about to lie, but then he saw the two yellow braids of his latest true love. The new girl was here at school! And right next to her was *the only empty seat* on the girls' side of the schoolhouse. He instantly spoke up.

"I STOPPED TO TALK WITH HUCKLEBERRY FINN!"

The schoolmaster thought the boy had lost his mind. So did the students.

"You—you did *what?*"

"Stopped to talk with Huckleberry Finn."

"Thomas Sawyer, this is the most foolish thing you could have said. Take off your jacket."

The schoolmaster gave Tom a whipping and ordered him to sit with the girls.

This had been Tom's plan all along. He sat down on the pine bench next to the girl with yellow hair.

Before long, Tom had given the girl a peach, drawn some pictures for her, and gotten her interested in him.

"You draw ever so nice—I wish I could draw," said the girl.

"It's easy," whispered Tom. "I'll teach you."

"Oh, will you? When?"

"At noon. Do you go home to eat?"

"I'll stay if you will."

"Good. What's your name?"

"Becky Thatcher. I'm Jeff's cousin. What's your name? Oh, I know. It's Thomas Sawyer."

"That's the name they whip me by. I'm Tom when I'm good. You call me Tom, will you?"

"Yes."

Now Tom began to scrawl some words on his tablet. The girl begged to see what he was writing.

"Oh, it ain't anything," said Tom, but he let her pull his arm away to get a peek.

When Becky saw the words "*I love you*" she said he was a bad boy and hit his hand. But she didn't look too unhappy.

At this point, the schoolmaster grabbed Tom by the ear and marched him back to his own seat. Although Tom's ear tingled, his heart was happy. He had a date with Becky at noon. Tom stared into his book and tried to study.

CHAPTER FOUR

Falling in Love – Failing in Love

Tom couldn't keep his mind on his book. He thought noon would never come—and tried to think of something to make the time go faster. His hand went into his pocket, and his face lit up when he felt the little box that held the tick bug he had gotten from Huck.

Before long, the bug was scampering back and forth on the top of Tom's desk. He and his friend Joe Harper were making a fun game of it. The boys were having a great old time when suddenly a tremendous whack came down on Tom's shoulders, and then another on Joe's. The schoolmaster had been watching—and their fun ended.

When noon finally came, Tom went straight to find Becky Thatcher. In a little while, Tom was teaching Becky to draw, and they began talking.

"Do you love rats?" he asked.

"No! I hate them!"

"Well, I do, too—*live* ones. But I mean *dead* ones, to swing round your head with a string."

"No, I don't care for rats much, either way. What I like is chewing gum," Becky answered.

"Oh, I should say so! I wish I had some now."

"Do you? I've got some. I'll let you chew it awhile, but you must give it back to me."

The two took turns passing the gum back and forth.

"Say, Becky, was you ever engaged?" asked Tom.

"What's that?"

"Why, engaged to be married."

"No."

"Would you like to?"

"I reckon so. I don't know. What is it like?"

"Like? Why it ain't like anything. You only just tell a boy you won't ever like anybody but him, ever, ever, ever. And then you kiss, and that's all. Anybody can do it."

Before long they were "engaged."

"Oh, it's so nice. I never heard of it before," said Becky.

"Oh, it's ever so fun!" agreed Tom. "Why, me and Amy Lawrence—"

Becky's big eyes told Tom that he had just made a big mistake.

"Oh, Tom! Then I ain't the first you've ever been engaged to!" she said, starting to cry.

"Oh, don't cry, Becky. I don't care for her anymore."

"Yes, you do, Tom—you know you do."

"Becky, I—I don't care for anybody but you."

No reply. Just sobs.

Tom got out his favorite treasure, a brass knob, and tried to give it to her to make up for his awful mistake.

"Please, Becky, won't you take it?"

She threw it to the floor. Tom left the school and decided not to come back for the rest of the day. Becky watched him disappear.

"Tom! Come back, Tom!"

She listened, but there was no answer. Her heart was broken.

Tom wandered around for a while, trying to think what he could do now to forget Becky. Should he run away? Should he become a clown in a circus? Or maybe he should become a soldier and a hero. No—better still, he would join the Indians and hunt buffaloes.

But no, there was something even better than this. He would be a pirate! That was it! How his name would make people shudder! He would sail the dancing seas in his black ship! And then he would suddenly appear in Sunday school in his black velvet coat, his great boots, his red sash, his great feathered hat, and his cutlass at his side! He would wave his flag with the skull and crossbones on it and hear the people whisper, "It's Tom Sawyer the Pirate!—the Black Avenger of the Spanish Main!"

Yes, that's what he would do! He would run away from home and start his new life the very next morning!

CHAPTER FIVE

The Graveyard – Murder!

Tom lay awake that night and waited for Huck's signal. The clock struck ten and then eleven. Finally, he heard a faint me-yow. He me-yow'd back as he climbed out his bedroom window and jumped to the ground. Huckleberry Finn was there—with his dead cat.

Before long, they were crawling through the high grass of the dark graveyard. A faint wind moaned through the trees. They found the new grave they were looking for, and hid under some elm trees. An owl hooted somewhere in the night.

"Say, Hucky—do you reckon old dead Hoss Williams hears us talking?" Tom whispered.

"O' course he does. Least his spirit does."

It was silent again for a time. Then Tom grabbed Huck's arm.

"Sh!"

"What is it, Tom?"

"Sh! There 'tis again! Didn't you hear it?"

"I—"

"There! Now you hear it?"

"Lord, Tom, they're coming! They're coming, sure. What'll we do?"

"I dunno. Think they'll see us?"

"Oh, Tom, them devils can see in the dark, same as cats. I wisht I hadn't come."

"Oh, don't be scared. If we keep perfectly still, maybe they won't notice us at all."

"I'll try to, Tom, but, Lord, I'm all shaky."

"Listen!"

The boys bent their heads together and hardly breathed. A faint sound of voices floated up from the far end of the graveyard.

"Look! See there!" whispered Tom. "What is it?"

"It's devil-fire. Oh, Tom, this is awful."

Some shadows came near—shadows swinging a tin lantern.

Huckleberry whispered with a shudder, "It's the devils sure enough. Three of 'em! Lordy, Tom, we're goners! Can you pray?"

"I'll try, but don't you worry. They ain't going to hurt us… Now I lay me down to sleep, I—"

"Sh!"

"What is it, Huck?"

"They're *humans!* One of 'em is ol' Muff Potter."

"No—'tain't so, is it?"

"Don't you move. He sounds like he's on the whiskey. He might not notice us."

"All right, I'll keep still. Say, Huck, I know another one of them voices. It's Injun Joe."

"That's so—that murderin' half-breed! I'd be happier if they *was* devils. What kin they be up to?"

The whispering stopped now, for the three men had reached the grave and stood within a few feet of the boys' hiding spot.

"Here it is," said a third voice.

The boys looked at each other in wonder—it was the voice of young Doctor Robinson! *He must be after a body for his medical studies.*

Potter and Injun Joe had a wheelbarrow with a rope and a couple of shovels on it. Soon they were digging up the grave. Finally a spade struck upon the coffin, and the men lifted it out onto the ground. They pried off the lid, got out the body and tied it on the wheelbarrow.

Potter took out a large knife, cut off the dangling end of the rope, and said, "Now the thing's ready, Doc, and you'll just pay another five dollars, or here it stays."

"That's the talk!" said Injun Joe.

"Look here, what does this mean?" said the doctor. "I've already paid you."

"Yes, and you done more than that," said Injun Joe. "Five years ago you drove me away from your father's kitchen one night, when I come to ask for something to eat. When I swore I'd get even with you if it took a hundred years, your father had me jailed. Did you think I'd forget? And now I've *got* you, and you got to settle up!"

He was threatening the doctor, with his fist in his face. The doctor struck out suddenly and put Injun Joe on the ground. Potter dropped his knife and exclaimed:

"Here, now, don't you hit my pard!"

In the next moment, Muff Potter had grabbed the doctor and the two were struggling. Injun Joe sprang to his feet, his eyes flaming. He snatched up Potter's knife, and went creeping, catlike and slinking, round and round the men. All at once the doctor got himself free, picked up the heavy headboard of Williams' grave, and knocked Potter to the ground with it—and in the same instant the Indian saw his chance and drove the knife into the young doctor's chest. Doctor Robinson staggered and fell on Muff Potter, dripping blood all over him. At that, the two frightened boys went running away in the dark.

Injun Joe stood over the two men. The doctor was dead.

"*That* score is settled—curse you," he muttered.

Then Injun Joe looked at Muff Potter and saw that he had been knocked out cold. He laid the knife in Potter's open right hand, and sat down on the coffin.

Potter began to stir and moan. His hand closed around the knife. He held it up, looked at it, and let it fall with a shudder. Then he sat up, pushing the body from him, not knowing what was going on.

"Lord, what's this, Joe?" he said.

"It's a dirty business," said Joe, without moving.

"What did you do it for, Joe?" asked Potter.

"I? I never done it! *You* done it, Muff Potter! You two was fighting, and he hit you with the headboard and you fell flat. Then you staggered up and shoved the knife in him."

"Oh, I don't remember a thing. It was all because of the whiskey, I reckon. Say you won't tell, Joc. You won't tell, *will* you, Joe?"

"No, I won't squeal on you."

"Oh, Joe, you're an angel." Potter began to cry.

"Come, now, that's enough of that. Let's get out of here. You go one way and I'll go another."

Potter started running. Injun Joe stood looking after him and thinking.

"If he's as confused from the crack on the head and the whiskey as I think he is, he'll forget his knife is still here."

Two or three minutes later, the only things left in the graveyard were the murdered man, the dug-up body of Hoss Williams, the coffin, the open grave—and Muff Potter's knife.

CHAPTER SIX

A Secret Oath – Signed in Blood

The two boys ran on and on toward the village, scared to death. At last, they burst through the door of an old empty building and fell exhausted on the floor.

"Huck, what do you suppose will happen?"

"If Doctor Robinson dies, I reckon there'll be a hanging."

Tom was thinking. "Who'll tell who done it? Us?"

"What are you talking about? S'pose something happened and Injun Joe didn't hang? Why, if we told, he'd kill us for sure. If anybody tells, let Muff Potter do it, if he's fool enough."

Tom said nothing—just went on thinking.

Presently Tom whispered, "Huck, Muff Potter don't know it. He'd just got that whack on the head when Injun Joe done it. He won't remember anything about it."

"By golly, that's so, Tom!"

"Hucky, you sure you can keep mum about what we seen?"

"Tom, we *got* to keep quiet. That devil Injun Joe would kill us for sure if we was to squeal 'bout this. Now, lookyhere, Tom, let's take hands and swear to one another—that's what we got to do—swear to each other that we'll never say a word."

"I'm agreed. It's the best thing. Should we just hold hands and swear that we—"

"Oh, no, that wouldn't do for this," said Huck. "There should be something in writing 'bout a big thing like this—a secret oath—signed in blood."

With that, Tom wrote out some fine words in red chalk on a piece of pine bark.

Then Tom took a needle from his jacket. Both boys pricked their thumbs and signed their initials in blood. They buried the bark and swore again to one another that they would never, ever tell a thing about what had gone on in the graveyard. Their lips were sealed!

Huck Finn and Tom Sawyer swears they will keep mum about this and they wish they may drop down dead in their tracks if they ever tell and they ever tell and rot.

TS HF

Tom crawled through his bedroom window and undressed as quietly as he could. He didn't know that Sid was still awake.

The next morning started out badly for Tom. Sid had told Aunt Polly that Tom had sneaked in late, and she was upset. Then, when Tom got to school, he got a whipping for skipping school the day before. And to make things even worse, Tom found something wrapped in paper on his desk. It was the brass knob he had given Becky. His heart was broken.

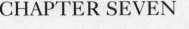

CHAPTER SEVEN

Muff Potter – Pirates – The Island

By noon that day, the whole village of St. Petersburg knew that Doctor Robinson had been killed with Muff Potter's knife. Everyone said that Muff Potter should be hung if they caught him.

All the villagers began to make their way to the graveyard. Tom and Huck were among them. Tom shivered from head to toe when he saw Injun Joe in the crowd.

As the Sheriff appeared over the hill leading someone, the people began shouting, "It's him! It's Muff Potter!"

The Sheriff came through the crowd with Muff Potter by the arm.

Muff's face and eyes showed his fear. When the poor fellow stood before the murdered man, he began shaking. He put his face in his hands and burst into tears.

"I didn't do it, friends," he sobbed. "Upon my word and honor, I never done it." Then he saw Injun Joe in the crowd. "Oh, Injun Joe, you promised me you'd never—"

"Is this your knife?" said the Sheriff, holding it in front of Muff.

Potter would have fallen if the crowd had not held him. He shuddered and hung his head as if he had given up.

"Tell 'em, Joe," Muff begged. "Tell 'em. It ain't any use anymore."

Huckleberry and Tom stood speechless as they heard Injun Joe lie about what had gone on. When they heard him say that Muff had done the killing, the boys wanted to break their oath and save poor innocent Muff. But they said nothing, not even when Injun Joe repeated the same lie at the courthouse, under oath.

Tom did not sleep well for the whole next week. His fear of Injun Joe and his guilt about keeping the awful secret were driving him crazy.

Every day or two, Tom went to the little jail-window and smuggled small treats through to Muff. This seemed to help his guilty feelings.

Tom began to feel sorry for himself after a while. He couldn't tell anyone his secret, and even his new girlfriend was mad at him. What was he to do? Then it came to him. Yes, they had forced him to it at last— he would lead the life of crime that he had thought about a week before, as a pirate on the high seas.

It just so happened that Tom's friend, Joe Harper, was ready to do something different, too. He had just gotten a beating from his mother for drinking some cream— and he hadn't even *tasted* it. So, when the two boys met, they were both ready to run away and find a new life.

Joe was for being a hermit and living on food scraps in a hidden cave. But after listening to Tom, he decided that it would be a lot more fun to be a pirate. The two pirates hunted up Huckleberry Finn, who agreed to join them.

First, they needed a hideout. They all agreed on Jackson's Island, since nobody lived there and it was only three miles down the Mississippi River from St. Petersburg. It was a small, wooded island that rose out of the water where the river was only about a mile wide. It lay just a swim away from the Illinois side. It was too far to swim to from their own Missouri side, but they could reach it by riding the current on a raft.

The three new pirates made plans to meet at midnight at a place on the riverbank above St. Petersburg where they knew a small log raft was kept. They aimed to capture the log raft and begin their life of crime on the high seas. Who would be their first victims, they didn't know.

About midnight, Tom arrived with a boiled ham and a few other things. Tom listened a moment, but heard not a sound. Then he gave a low whistle. From somewhere below, a cautious voice said:

"Who goes there?"

"Tom Sawyer, the Black Avenger of the Spanish Main. Name your names."

"Huck Finn the Red-Handed, and Joe Harper the Terror of the Seas." Tom had come up with these names from some of his favorite stories.

"All is well. Give the password."

Two hoarse whispers delivered the same awful word:

"BLOOD!"

The Terror of the Seas had brought a slab of bacon. Finn the Red-Handed had stolen a frying pan. The Black Avenger of the Spanish Main said it would never do to start without some fire. So, they helped themselves to a live coal left over from the fire of some campers who had gone off to town.

They shoved off on the little raft. Tom shouted out orders to the crew which none of them understood, including Tom. But they sounded real "pirate-like" and important.

"Luff, and bring her to the wind!"

"Aye-aye, sir!"

"Steady, steady-y-y-y!"

"Steady it is, sir!"

"Let her go off a point!"

"Point it is, sir!"

"Up the mainsail! Down the jigsa'll! Port the mizz'nmast 'round to starboard, me mates!"

After Tom ran out of make-believe orders, the crew quieted down and the raft floated on down the Mississippi. Soon they were passing in front of St. Petersburg. Tom wished Becky could see him now, facing death on the wild seas.

About two o'clock in the morning they reached the sandy shore of Jackson's Island. They waded back and forth, carrying their things to land. There was part of an old sail on the little raft, and this they spread as a tent to cover their food. But they would sleep in the open air in good weather, for this is what outlaws did.

They made a fire using the live coal they had brought. After a supper of bacon, the boys stretched themselves out on the grass, filled with happiness.

"Ain't it great?" said Joe.

"It's *wild*," said Tom. "What would the boys say if they could see us?"

"Say? Well, they'd just die to be here—hey, Hucky?"

"I reckon so," said Huckleberry. "Anyways, I'm happy. I don't want nothing better'n this."

"It's just the life for me," said Tom. "You don't have go to school, and wash, and all that foolishness."

Gradually the talk stopped, and the little pirates got sleepy. The corncob pipe dropped from the fingers of the Red-Handed. The Terror of the Seas and the Black Avenger of the Spanish Main said their prayers to themselves, and within minutes, all three were sound asleep.

Tom woke the other pirates in the morning, and in a minute or two they had their clothes off and were splashing in the river. When they got back to camp, Joe sliced some bacon for breakfast while Tom and Huck caught a few small fish. They fried the fish with the bacon. No breakfast had ever tasted better.

They went off through the woods to do some exploring. It was late afternoon when they got back to camp and sat down in the shade to talk. But the talk soon died out, and they all began thinking quietly to themselves. Each of them was feeling homesick, but they were ashamed to say so. All of a sudden, they heard a large boom in the distance.

"What is it?!" cried Joe.

"Hush!" said Tom. "Listen."

The same boom came again.

They sprang to their feet and hurried to the shore for a look. The little steam ferryboat was about a mile below St. Petersburg, her deck crowded with people. Suddenly, a great puff of white smoke burst from the ferryboat's side, and the same boom sounded again.

"I know now!" exclaimed Tom. "Somebody's drownded! They're lookin' for him in the river."

"That's it!" said Huck. "They shoot a cannon over the water to make the body rise."

"By jings, I wish I was over there now," said Joe.

"I do, too," said Huck. "I'd give heaps to know who it is."

Tom was thinking hard. "Boys," he said, "I know who's drownded—it's *us!*"

They felt like heroes in an instant. People might even be feeling sorry for the times they had been unkind to them. It was great to be a pirate, after all.

As evening came, the boats stopped searching, and the pirates returned to camp. When darkness came, they stopped talking and gazed into the fire. The excitement was gone now, and Joe could not help but think of the people at home who might be sad and worried. He asked what the others thought about going back home. Tom made fun of him, and Huck went along with Tom.

That night, when the others were asleep, Tom left the boys a note on some sycamore bark. He wrote another note, which he rolled up and stuck in his pocket. Then he secretly tiptoed through the trees toward the river.

CHAPTER EIGHT

Sneaking Ashore – The Funerals

Tom knew he couldn't steer the raft upstream against the current. So he began wading the shallow waters that led to the Illinois side. He swam the remaining hundred yards to shore, and then hiked his way north. Shortly before ten o'clock, he reached the Illinois ferrylanding that lay just across from St. Petersburg, Missouri. He saw the ferryboat lying in the shadow of the trees and the high bank. *Good!* he thought. *It hasn't left yet for its final crossing of the night.*

Everything was silent under the blinking stars. Tom slipped quietly into the little skiff tied to the ferryboat's side and hid there during the crossing.

When the ferryboat pulled up to the dock near St. Petersburg, Tom slid into the water and swam to shore. Then he ran along the back streets of the village, and soon found himself at his aunt's back fence. He climbed over and peeked through a window into Aunt Polly's bedroom. There sat Aunt Polly, Sid, Mary, and Joe Harper's mother, talking. They were by the bed, and the bed was between them and the door. Tom cracked open the door and was able to slip into the room and crawl under the bed without being seen.

"He warn't *bad*—only mischievous," Aunt Polly was saying. "And he was the best-hearted boy that ever was"—and she began to cry.

"It was just the same with my Joe," said Mrs. Harper. "He was full of his devilment, but he was just as unselfish and kind as he could be. Lordy me, to think I went and whipped him for taking that cream, never once remembering that I had thrown it out myself because it was sour." Mrs. Harper cried as if her heart would break.

"Oh, Mrs. Harper, I don't know how to give him up!" cried Aunt Polly.

Soon Tom was crying, too—feeling mighty sorry for himself.

Tom went on listening and found out that everyone believed the boys might have drowned in the river. This was Wednesday night. If the bodies were still missing on Sunday, the village would hold the boys' funerals. Tom shivered.

Finally, Mrs. Harper left, sobbing. Sid and Mary went off to bed.

Aunt Polly knelt down and prayed for Tom with so much love that he was soon crying his eyes out again.

When Aunt Polly was asleep, Tom slipped from under the bed and stood looking at her. He was going to leave the note he had written, but then a more exciting idea came to him. He put the note back into his pocket, gave his sweet Auntie a light kiss, and then sneaked out the door.

Tom made his way back to the ferrylanding. He untied the little skiff from the ferryboat, paddled his way across the river and left the skiff at the Illinois-side ferrylanding. He had half a mind to keep the skiff, since he was a pirate, but he knew there'd be a search for it. Instead he hiked back down the wooded Illinois shoreline, swam across to the island, and waded to shore.

He sat down and took a long rest just outside the camp. When the sun was coming up, he crept in close and could hear Joe and Huck talking.

"No, Tom's true-blue, Huck, and he'll come back. He won't leave us. He knows that would be a disgrace to a pirate. He's up to something. His note says if he ain't back by morning, to go ahead and have breakfast."

"And here he is!" shouted Tom, jumping out of the bushes.

After a big breakfast of bacon and fish, Tom told his story. They all felt like proud heroes when they knew how much they were missed.

The three pirates had an exciting time over the next couple of days, but thoughts of home kept coming back to them. Tom even found himself writing "*Becky*" in the sand with his big toe.

By now, Joe was so homesick that he could hardly stand it. Huck was sad, too. Tom felt the same way, but tried hard not to show it. He had a plan that he wanted to keep a secret for now, but if things didn't cheer up, he might have to tell them soon. He tried to brighten Joe and Huck up with the idea of a treasure hunt.

"I bet there's been pirates on this island before, boys. How'd you feel about finding a rotten chest full of gold and silver—hey?"

But the two boys showed little interest. Joe sat poking the sand with a stick, looking very gloomy.

"Oh, boys," said Joe, "let's give it up. I want to go home. It's so lonesome."

"Oh, no, Joe. You'll feel better before long," said Tom. "Just think of the fishing and swimming that's here."

"They ain't no good. I don't seem to care for things, somehow, when there ain't anybody to tell me I can't do 'em. I want to go home," said Joe, and began packing his things.

"I want to go, too, Tom," said Huck.

"Well, go 'long—who's holdin' you back?"

Huck took his clothes and started off with Joe.

Tom stood looking after him, thinking. All at once, he ran yelling after his friends.

"Wait! Wait! I want to tell you something!"

They stopped, and Tom let them in on his secret plan. As soon as they heard it, they let out a whoop of joy. The boys came happily back and began their games again, chattering all the time about Tom's neat plan.

Around midnight, the worst thunderstorm the boys had ever seen ripped through the camp. The thunder was like an army of cannons, and the lightning made the woods as bright as day. The wind tore away their little sail-tent, and the terrified boys fled through the rain to a great oak near the riverbank. Here they huddled, shivering from the cold and the exploding thunder. Trees crashed to the ground. The river drenched them in its wild spray. It only lasted about thirty minutes, but it seemed like hours to the three brave pirates. At last, things quieted down, and they dropped off into a wet, exhausted sleep.

Whether it was the storm or what, Tom didn't know, but the next morning he saw that Joe and Huck were homesick again. Tom tried to cheer them up and got them interested in playing Indians. It wasn't long before they were stripped to their shorts and striped from head to toe with black mud. The three Indians, all chiefs of course, went tearing off through the woods to attack an English village.

We will leave them for now to laugh and brag and count their captives.

There was no laughing in the little village that same Saturday afternoon. St. Petersburg was strangely quiet. Mrs. Harper and Aunt Polly both cried themselves to sleep that night as they thought about the next day.

The little church was full Sunday morning for the funerals of the three boys. The minister spread his hands and prayed. A moving hymn was sung, and the Bible verse followed: "I am the Resurrection and the Life."

A moment later, the church door creaked. The minister raised his crying eyes and could not believe what he saw. All at once, everyone in the church stood and stared while the three *dead* boys came marching in. They had been hiding in back, listening to their own funeral sermon!

Aunt Polly, Mary, and the Harpers hugged and kissed their boys, while poor Huck stood alone. He started to sneak away, but Tom grabbed him.

"Aunt Polly, it ain't fair. Somebody's got to be glad to see Huck."

"You're right, Tom," said his aunt. "I'm glad to see him, poor motherless thing!" And the loving hugs that Aunt Polly gave him made Huck feel even worse than he had before.

Everybody began to sing thanks to God. It shook the whole church. Tom Sawyer the Pirate looked around and noticed how the other children looked up to him in admiration. This was the proudest moment of his life.

Tom got more spanks and kisses that day—depending on how Aunt Polly felt at the time—than he had gotten before in a year.

CHAPTER NINE

Taking the Heat – Winning the Heart

That had been Tom's great secret—the plan to return home with his brother pirates and attend their own funerals. They had paddled over to the Missouri shore on their log raft and landed five or six miles below St. Petersburg. They had slept in the woods at the edge of the village the night before, and then sneaked into a room at the back of the church early Sunday morning.

What a hero Tom was now! At school the next day, the children made so much of Tom and Joe that the two heroes became "stuck-up." They began to tell their adventures—and the more they told, the more they made up and added to the story.

Tom decided that he no longer needed to chase after Becky Thatcher. Now that he was a hero, maybe she'd want to "make up." When Becky arrived at school, Tom pretended not to see her. Before long, Becky started watching Tom out of the corner of her eye and noticed that he was talking more to Amy Lawrence than anyone else. She was jealous and a little angry. She got closer to Tom and began speaking loudly to one of the girls.

"Why, Mary Austin, I'm glad to see you. I wanted to tell you about my picnic."

"Oh, that's jolly. When is it going to be?"

"In a little while. Maybe around vacation time."

"Oh, won't it be fun! You going to have all the girls and boys?"

"Yes, everyone that's friends to me—or wants to be." She sneaked a peek at Tom, but he kept on talking to Amy Lawrence.

Soon all the children were begging to come to the picnic, except Tom and Amy. Tom turned coolly away, and took Amy with him. Tears came to Becky's eyes.

Tom ran home at noon. He could not take any more. How could Becky stay so mad at him? Why was *he* acting so mean, too?

He returned to school after lunch with a heavy heart—until he was lucky enough to spot Becky Thatcher on the way. He ran to her and said:

"I acted mighty mean today, Becky, and I'm so sorry. I won't ever, ever do that way again. Please make up, won't you?"

The girl stopped and looked at him angrily.

"I'll thank you to keep yourself *to* yourself, Mr. Thomas Sawyer. I'll never speak to you again."

She tossed her head and left.

Poor girl, she did not know how she would regret her words that very day.

The teacher, Mr. Dobbins, had always wanted to be a doctor. He still took out a medical book every day and read it when the students were working. He kept the book locked up, and every child in the school wanted to see what was inside it. Now, as Becky was passing by the desk, she noticed that the drawer was open, unlocked! This was her chance. She reached in and pulled out the "secret" book. The title page (Professor Somebody's *Anatomy*) meant nothing to her, so she began to turn the pages. She came to a page that had a picture of a person—with no clothes on!

At that moment, Tom stepped in the door and saw her. Becky grabbed at the book to close it, and had the bad luck to tear the page right down the middle. She stuffed the book back into the desk and burst out crying with shame.

"Tom Sawyer, you are just as mean as you can be, to sneak up on me. You ought to be ashamed of yourself. You know you're going to tattle-tale on me, and oh, I'll be whipped, and I never was whipped in school."

Then she stamped her little foot and hurried to her desk.

A whole hour drifted by. And then it happened. Mr. Dobbins unlocked his desk and reached for his book. Tom shot a look at Becky. She looked helpless and scared. Tom forgot about his anger with her. Quick—something must be done to help her. He thought he could grab the book and fly out the door, but it was too late—the teacher was already turning the pages! There was no help for Becky now, he thought.

The teacher stood up, a look of anger in his eyes. "Who tore this book?" he shouted.

There was not a sound. Mr. Dobbins started questioning each child.

Soon Mr. Dobbins came to Becky Thatcher. Tom was trying to think what to do.

"Rebecca Thatcher!" (Tom glanced at her face—it was white with terror.) "Did you tear this book?"

A new idea shot like lightning through Tom's brain. He sprang to his feet and shouted:

"I done it!"

The loving looks of thanks in Becky's eyes made the whipping Tom got worthwhile. Becky met him after school and told him she was sorry for saying she'd never speak to him again. Tom forgave her, and fell asleep that night with Becky's last words ringing in his ears—

"Tom, how *could* you be so good and kind!"

Tom was happy, not only because of Becky, but also because school was just about done for the year, and summer vacation would soon begin.

CHAPTER TEN

The Murder Trial – Facing Injun Joe

School hadn't been out for long when Tom started to get a little bored. Becky had gone away to her summer home, and he was running out of things to do.

He tried keeping a diary, but nothing happened for three days, so he gave it up. The first of the traveling shows came to town. Tom and Joe Harper got up a band of performers and were happy for two days.

A circus came. The boys played circus for three days afterward in tents made of rag carpeting—ticket price was three pins for boys, two for girls—and then circusing was given up.

Just when Tom was running out of ideas, the sleepy summer became a lot more exciting when Muff Potter's murder trial began. It was the talk of the village. Tom could not get away from it. It kept him in a cold shiver all the time. He met alone with Huck to be sure he had said nothing about that awful night in the graveyard.

"Huck, have you ever told anybody about—that?"

"Oh—course I haven't. What makes you ask?"

"Well, I was scared."

"Why, Tom Sawyer, we wouldn't have been alive two days if we'd told. *You* know that."

Tom felt better.

"Huck, nobody could get you to tell, could they?"

"Get me to tell? Why would I tell and have Injun Joe kill me?"

"Well, that's all right, then. I reckon we're safe as long as we keep our mouths shut," said Tom.

"Me too. I reckon old Muff's a goner, though. I feel sorry for him, sometimes. He don't amount to much, but he ain't ever done anything to hurt anybody. Just fishes a little and loafs around a lot. But he's kind of good—he give me half a fish once."

"Well, he's fixed kites for me, Huck, and tied fishin' hooks to my line. I wish we could get him out of there, 'specially since he never done the murder."

As the twilight came, the boys went, as they had before, to the jail cell and gave Potter some treats. Muff was so thankful and kind to them that Tom felt more guilty than ever about keeping the secret.

For two days Tom hung around outside the courtroom. Things were looking very bad for Muff Potter. At the end of the second day, the talk was that Injun Joe's story about the killing would bring a guilty verdict from the jury the very next day. Tom wondered what he should do.

The whole village was at the courthouse the next morning. The jury came in and took their places. Shortly afterward, Potter was brought in with chains around him, and he was seated where Injun Joe could stare right at him. The judge and the lawyers arrived and began to call witnesses.

Every one of the witnesses swore to facts that made it sound as though Muff had done the killing. Muff's lawyer didn't even *bother* to question the witnesses! Nobody, including the judge, understood what Muff's lawyer might be up to. Finally, when it looked as though Muff was sure to be framed for the murder, his lawyer stood and began to speak.

"Your Honor, we said at the opening of this trial that we would prove that our client did this terrible thing in a moment of insanity while drunk. We have changed our mind. We are changing our plea to *not guilty!*" Turning to the clerk, he said, "Call Thomas Sawyer to the stand!"

The whole courtroom was shocked and puzzled, including Muff Potter. Every eye watched as Tom took a seat before the judge and swore to tell the truth.

"Thomas Sawyer, where were you on the seventeenth of June, about the hour of midnight?"

Tom glanced at Injun Joe's mean face, and his tongue wouldn't work. After a few moments, the boy got a little of his strength back, and answered weakly, "In the graveyard!"

A hateful smile flitted across Injun Joe's face.

"Were you near Hoss Williams's grave?"

"Yes, sir."

"Were you hidden, or not?"

"I was hid behind the elm trees that's on the edge of the grave."

Injun Joe sat up in his seat.

"Anyone with you?"

"Yes, sir. I went there with—"

"Wait—wait a moment. Never mind the other name. We will call him as a witness later. Did you carry anything there with you?"

Tom hesitated and looked confused.

"Speak out, my boy. The truth is always best. What did you take there?"

"Only a—a—dead cat."

There was a ripple of laughter, which the court put a stop to.

"We will produce the skeleton of that cat," smiled Muff's lawyer. "Now, my boy, tell us everything that happened—tell it in your own way—don't skip anything, and don't be afraid."

Tom began, and every eye was on him as the audience heard the terrible tale. Every person was on the edge of his seat as Tom said:

"—and as the doctor knocked Muff Potter down with the headboard, Injun Joe jumped with the knife and—"

Crash! Quick as lightning, Injun Joe sprang for a window, tore his way through all who tried to stop him, and was gone!

CHAPTER ELEVEN

A Hero – Digging for Hidden Treasure

Tom was a hero once more. The villagers were now as nice to Muff Potter as they had been mean to him before.

Tom's days were wonderful, but his nights were times of horror. Injun Joe was in all his dreams. Poor Huck was in the same state of terror when he found out Tom had told the whole story to the lawyer the night before the trial. Huck was afraid that *his* part in the thing might leak out. At least Injun Joe's escape had saved Huck from having to testify in court! But Huck had lost faith in people when Tom couldn't keep a secret—even after Tom and Huck had sworn their secret oath.

Rewards had been offered and the countryside was searched, but no Injun Joe was found. The days drifted on, and each day helped to take away a little of Tom's fear. He began to think of new ways to stay busy and have fun. He decided to do what every normal boy wants to do sometime in his life—dig for hidden treasure!

Tom found Huck and laid out his plans. Huck was always willing to try anything that sounded fun and required no money.

"Where'll we dig?" said Huck.

"Oh, most anywhere."

"Why, is it hid all around?"

"No, indeed it ain't. It's hid in mighty special places, Huck."

"Who hides it?"

"Why, robbers, of course—who'd you reckon? Sunday school teachers?"

"Don't they come after it anymore?"

"No, they *think* they will, but they generally forget the directions to it, or else they die. Anyway, it lays there a long time and gets rusty, and then somebody finds an old yellow paper that tells where to find it."

"Have you got one of them papers, Tom?"

"No."

"Well, then, how you going to find the clues?"

"I don't need any. They always bury it under a haunted house or on an island, or under a dead tree where the shadow of its one limb falls at midnight."

"Is it under all of them?"

"How you talk! No!"

"Then how you going to know which one to go for?"

"Go for all of 'em!"

"Why, Tom, it'll take all summer."

"Well, what of that? Suppose you find a rotten chest with a hundred dollars in it?"

"That's good enough for me! But say, where you going to dig first?"

"Well, I don't know. S'pose we try that old dead-limb tree on the hill t'other side of Still-House Creek?"

"I'm agreed."

So they got a broken pick-axe and a shovel, and began their three-mile hike. When they arrived, they threw themselves down in the shade of a tree to rest.

"I like this," said Tom.

"So do I."

"Say, Huck, if we find a treasure here, what you going to do with your share?"

"Well, I'll have pie and a glass of soda every day, and I'll go to every circus that comes along. What you going to do with your'n, Tom?"

"I'm going to buy a new drum, and a sure-'nuff sword, and a red necktie, and a dog, and get married."

"Married?"

"That's it."

"Tom, you—why, you ain't in your right mind."

"Wait—you'll see."

"What's the name of the gal?"

"It ain't a gal at all—it's a girl."

"It's all the same, I reckon. Some says gal, some says girl. Anyway, what's her name, Tom?"

"I'll tell you maybe—later on. Now forget about this and we'll go to digging."

They worked and sweated for half an hour. Nothing. They dug another half-hour. Still no luck.

Huck said, "Do they always bury it as deep as this?"

"Sometimes—not always. I reckon we haven't got the right place."

So they chose a new spot and began again. Finally Huck leaned on his pick-axe, wiped the sweat from his face and said:

"Where you going to dig next, after we get this one?"

"I reckon maybe we'll try the old tree that's over yonder on Cardiff Hill back of the Widow Douglas's mansion."

"I reckon that'll be a good one."

The work went on. After a while Huck said, "Dern it, we must be in the wrong place again. What do you think?"

"It is mighty strange, Huck, but I think I know what the matter is! What fools we are! You got to find out where the shadow of the limb falls at midnight, and *that's* where you dig!"

"Shucks! We've fooled away all this work for nothing. Now hang it all, we got to come back in the night. Can you get out?"

"You bet! We've got to do it tonight, too, because if somebody sees these holes they'll know in a minute what's here, and they'll go for it."

"Well, I'll come around and me-yow tonight."

"All right. Let's hide the tools in the bushes."

The boys were there that night somewhere around midnight. They marked where the shadow fell, and began to dig. The hole got deeper and deeper.

At last Tom said, "It ain't any use, Huck. We're wrong again."

"Well, but we *can't* be wrong. We spotted the shadow exactly."

"I know it, but then there's another thing."

"What's that?"

"Why, we only guessed at the time. Probably it wasn't dead-on midnight."

Huck dropped his shovel. "Say, Tom, let's give this place up, and try somewheres else."

"All right, I reckon we better. Let's try the haunted house."

"Dern it, I don't like haunted houses, Tom. Why, that's just where ghosts come sliding around and peep over your shoulder."

"Yes, but, Huck, ghosts only travel around at night. They won't stop us from digging there in the daytime."

"Well, that's so. We'll try that haunted house in the daytime if you say so, but I reckon it's taking chances."

They had started down the hill by this time. There in the middle of the moonlit valley below them stood the "haunted" house, all alone, weeds covering the doorsteps, the windows broken, a corner of the roof caved in. The boys stayed well away from it and went home through the woods on the rear side of Cardiff Hill.

CHAPTER TWELVE

Hiding Above – Gold Below

The next day the boys were heading toward the woods when they remembered it was Friday. It was bad luck to be fooling around with ghosts on a Friday, so they decided to play Robin Hood for the rest of the day. Lots of rich people were robbed, and lots of money given to the poor by a make-believe band of merry men.

On Saturday, shortly after noon, the boys picked up their tools at the dead tree and headed for the haunted house. They crept to the door and took a trembling peek, only to see a huge room full of hanging cobwebs. An old crumbling fireplace stood on one wall near a broken-down staircase.

Soon they were inside, talking in whispers.

In a little while, seeing no ghosts and getting braver, they threw their tools into a corner and went up the rickety old stairs. Finding nothing in an empty closet, they were about to go back downstairs and begin digging when—

"Sh!" said Tom.

"What is it?" whispered Huck, frightened.

"Sh! ... There! ... Hear it?"

"Yes! ... Oh, my! Let's run!"

"Keep still! Don't you move! They're coming right toward the door."

The boys stretched themselves on the floor and looked through a hole in the floor, scared to death.

Two men entered. Tom whispered, "There's the old deaf and dumb Spaniard that's been nosin' around town lately—never seen the other man before."

The "other man" was a ragged creature with a mean face. The Spaniard, wrapped in a colorful cape, had bushy white whiskers and long white hair that flowed from under his sombrero. The ragged man was speaking:

"No," he said, "I've thought it all over, and I don't like it. It's dangerous."

"Dangerous! Nonsense!" grunted the "deaf and dumb" Spaniard—to the surprise of the boys, because if he was deaf and dumb, how could he hear and talk?

The Spaniard's voice made the boys gasp and shake with fear. It was Injun Joe's!

"What's any more dangerous than that job up yonder?" he growled. "But nothing's come of it."

"That's different. It was way up the river with nobody around. It won't ever be known that we tried, anyway, since we didn't succeed."

"Well, what's more dangerous than coming here in the daytime?!—anybody would suspect us that saw us."

"I know that. But there warn't any other place as handy after that fool of a job. I want to get out of this house. I wanted to yesterday, only it warn't any use trying to stir out of here, with those boys playing over there on the hill right in front of us."

Tom and Huck shook again when they heard this, and thought how lucky it was that they had remembered it was Friday and decided to wait a day.

After a long silence Injun Joe said, "Look here, you go back up the river where you belong. Wait there till you hear from me. I'll take the chances on dropping into this town just once more, for a look. We'll do that 'dangerous' job after I've snooped around a little and think things look better for it. Then we'll get out of here and head for Texas. Now, I'm going to get some sleep! It's your turn to watch."

The "Spaniard" was soon snoring. It wasn't very long before the other man had also fallen asleep.

The boys drew a long, grateful breath. Tom whispered, "Now's our chance—come."

But just then, one snore stopped. Injun Joe sat up, looked around, and stirred his partner awake with his foot.

"Here, you're a fine watchman, ain't you! Nearly time for us to be moving, pard. What'll we do with the stolen loot we've got left?"

"I don't know—leave it here as we've always done, I reckon. No use to take it away till we start south. Six hundred and fifty in silver's a lot to carry."

Tom and Huck looked at each other with wide eyes and open mouths.

"Well—all right—it won't hurt to come here once more and get it," said Injun Joe.

"No—but I'd say come in the night as we used to do—it's better," said the partner.

"Yes, but it may be a good while before I get the right chance at that other job. Accidents might happen. It ain't in such a very good place. We better bury it—and bury it deep."

"Good idea," said the partner. He walked across the room, knelt down, raised one of the stones in the fireplace and took out a bag that jingled nicely. He passed the bag to Joe, who was on his knees, digging with his knife.

The boys forgot all their fears in an instant. With greedy eyes they watched every movement. Luck! Here was the best kind of treasure hunting—they would know right where to dig!

Then Joe's knife struck something.

"What is it?" said his partner.

"Half-rotten board—no, it's a box," replied Injun Joe.

He reached his hand in and drew it out—

"Man, it's money!"

The two men pulled out several gold coins. The boys above were just as excited as the men below.

"We'll make quick work of this," said the ragged partner. "There's an old rusty pick-axe over among the weeds in the corner."

He ran and grabbed the boys' pick-axe and shovel. Injun Joe took the pick-axe, looked it over, and began digging. The box was soon out of the ground. The men stared at the treasure.

"Pard, there's thousands of dollars here," said Injun Joe.

"It was always said that Murrel's gang used to hang around here one summer," the ragged man said.

"I know it," said Injun Joe, "and this looks like some of their old loot."

"*Now* you won't need to do that *other* job."

Injun Joe frowned.

"You don't know me. And you don't know all that's behind the reason for that other job. It ain't only robbery—it's *revenge!*" A wicked light flamed in his eyes. "I'll need your help in it. When it's finished—then Texas. Go home to your Nance and your kids, and stand by till you hear from me."

"Well—if you say so. What'll we do with this— bury it again?" said the partner.

"Yes. [*There was great delight overhead.*] No! [*There was great distress overhead.*] I'd nearly forgot. That pick-axe had fresh earth on it! [*The boys became sick with terror.*] Why would there be a pick and a shovel here with fresh dirt on them? Who brought them here—and where have they gone? Have you heard anybody?—seen anybody? What!—bury it again and leave them to come and see the ground dug up? Not a chance. We'll take it to my den," said Injun Joe.

"Why, of course! Might have thought of that before. You mean Number One?"

"No—Number Two—under the cross. The other place is bad—too common."

"All right. It's nearly dark enough to start."

They slipped out of the house in the twilight, and moved toward the river with their box of treasure.

Tom and Huck stood up, weak but thankful, and stared after them through the cracks between the logs of the house.

The two boys did not talk much as they made their way down the hill toward town. They were thinking what bad luck it was, leaving the shovel and the pick there. Except for that, Injun Joe would have hidden the silver with the gold right there until his "revenge job" was taken care of, and then he would have returned and found that the money was missing. Bad, bad luck that the tools were ever brought there!

They decided to keep a lookout for that "Spaniard" when he came to town looking for chances to do his "revenge job," and follow him to den "Number Two," wherever that might be. Then Tom had a horrible thought.

"Revenge? What if he means *us*, Huck?!"

"Oh, don't say that!" said Huck, nearly fainting.

They talked it all over and agreed to believe that Injun Joe might possibly mean somebody else—at least that he might mean nobody but Tom, since Tom was the only one of them that Injun Joe had seen at Muff Potter's trial.

It wasn't much comfort to Tom to be the only one in danger! Having a little company would be an improvement, he thought.

CHAPTER THIRTEEN

On Watch – In Room 2

After a quick breakfast the next morning, Tom went toward town and found Huck dangling his legs over a flatboat, looking forlorn.

"Hello, Huck! Why so sad?"

"Tom, if we'd-a left the dern tools at the dead tree, we'd-a got the money. Oh, ain't it awful!"

"Huck, we gotta track them to find that money."

"Tom, we'll never find Injun Joe. I'd feel mighty shaky if I was to see him, anyway."

"Well, so'd I, but I'd like to track him down to his Number Two hideout."

"Number Two—yes, that's it. I been thinkin' 'bout that. What do you reckon it is?"

"I dunno. Say, Huck—maybe it's the number of a house!"

"Goody! ... No, Tom, that ain't it. If it is, it ain't in this little town. Ain't no house numbers here."

"Well, that's so. Lemme think a minute. Maybe it's the number of a room—in a tavern, you know!"

"Oh, that's the trick! There ain't but two taverns. We can find out quick."

"You stay here, Huck, till I come back."

Tom was off at once. He found that, in the best tavern, Room 2 was rented by a young lawyer. In the other tavern, Room 2 was a mystery. The tavern-keeper's young son said it was kept locked all the time, and he never saw anybody go into it or come out of it, except at night. He said he had noticed that there was a light in there the night before. Tom rushed back and told Huck.

"That's what I've found out, Huck. I reckon that's the very Number Two we're after."

"I reckon it is, Tom. Now what you going to do?"

"I'll tell you. The back door of that Room Two is the door that comes out into that little alley between the tavern and the old brick store. Now, you get hold of all the door keys you can find, and I'll snitch all of Auntie's, and the first dark night

we'll go there and try 'em. And be sure you keep a lookout for Injun Joe, because he said he was going to drop into town and spy around once more for a chance to get his revenge. If you see him, you just follow him. If he don't go to that Room Two, that ain't the place."

"Lordy, I don't want to foller him by myself!"

"Why, it'll be night, sure. He might not ever see you—and if he did, maybe he'd never think anything."

"Well, if it's pretty dark I reckon I'll track him. I'll try."

"Now you're *talking!* Don't you ever weaken, Huck, and I won't."

Three nights later, Thursday, was the first dark night with no moon. An hour before midnight, the tavern closed up and its lights were put out. Nobody had entered or left the alley.

Tom got his lantern, and the two boys crept forward in the gloom. Huck stood watch and Tom felt his way toward the tavern. After what seemed like hours, there was a sudden flash of light, and Tom came tearing by him.

"Run!" he said. "Run for your life!"

The boys never stopped till they reached a shed at the lower end of the village. As soon as Tom got his breath he said:

"Huck, it was awful! I didn't need the keys. The door was unlocked and I walked right in! Then…"

"What!—what'd you see, Tom?"

"Huck, I 'most stepped onto Injun Joe's hand!"

"No!"

"Yes! He was lying there, sound asleep on the floor."

"Lordy, what did you do? Did he wake up?"

"No, never moved. Drunk, I reckon. I just got out of there!"

"Say, Tom, did you see that box?"

"Huck, I didn't wait to look around. I didn't see the box. I didn't see the cross. I didn't see anything but a bottle and a tin cup on the floor by Injun Joe, and a whole bunch more whiskey bottles around."

"Say, Tom, now's a mighty good time to get that box if Injun Joe's drunk."

"Right! *You* try it!"

Huck shuddered. "Well, no—I reckon not."

"And I reckon not, Huck. Lookyhere, let's not try that thing again till we know Injun Joe's not in there. It's too scary. Now, if we watch every night, we'll be dead sure to see him go out, some time or other, and then we'll snatch that box quicker'n lightning."

"Well, I'm agreed. I'll watch the whole night long every night if you'll do the other part of the job."

"All right, I will. All you got to do is to run up Hooper Street a block and me-yow—and if I'm asleep, you throw some gravel at the window and that'll get me up."

"Agreed!"

"Now, Huck, I'll go home. It'll begin to be daylight in a couple of hours. You go back and watch that long, will you?"

"I said I would, Tom, and I will. I'll sleep all day in Ben Rogers' hay barn, and I'll stand watch all night."

"Well, I won't need you in the daytime, Huck. I'll let you sleep. Whenever you see something's up during the night, just skip right around and me-yow."

CHAPTER FOURTEEN

McDougal's Cave – Huck the Spy

The first thing Tom heard on Friday morning was good news—Judge Thatcher's family had come back to town, and Becky had talked her mother into having the picnic the next day. Tom was so exited about the treasure and seeing Becky again he could barely sleep that night.

Morning came, and a happy group of children was gathered at Judge Thatcher's. Several young men and ladies went along as guardians. Soon the cheery crowd headed down Main Street toward the old steam ferryboat which had been rented for the day. Sid was sick and had to miss the fun. Cousin Mary remained at home to entertain him.

The last thing Mrs. Thatcher said to Becky was: "You'll not get back till late. Perhaps you'd better stay all night with some of the girls that live near the ferrylanding, child."

"Then I'll stay with Susy Harper, Mamma," Becky had said.

"Very well. And don't get into any trouble."

Three miles below town the ferryboat stopped. The crowd went ashore and the forest and hills were full of screams and laughter. After a picnic feast, somebody shouted:

"Who wants to explore McDougal's Cave?"

Everybody did! They all grabbed candles and headed up the hillside to a large cave with lots of underground rooms and tunnels. Most of the young men knew a part of it, but it was still easy to get turned around and lost in this dark, crooked cave. It was said that one might wander days and nights in its tangle of tunnels and pits and never find the end of it. Tom Sawyer knew as much of the cave as anyone.

Time flew by as the happy boys and girls chased each other around the tunnels of the cave. It was almost night when most of them returned to the boat.

Meanwhile, Huck was already on his watch. Eleven o'clock came and the tavern lights were put out. Huck waited what seemed a long time, but nothing happened.

Then he heard a noise. The next moment two men brushed by him, and one seemed to have something under his arm. It must be that box! So they were going to remove the treasure. Why call Tom now? It would be silly—the men would get away with the box and never be found again. No, he would follow them.

They moved through the streets and took the road past the old Welshman's house that led to the top of Cardiff Hill. There they disappeared into a narrow path, hidden by bushes. Huck got closer, afraid he had lost them. He was about to start running, when a man cleared his throat not four feet from him! Huck's heart shot into his throat, but he swallowed it again. He saw that he was within five steps of the stone wall entrance to Widow Douglas's place. *Very well*, he thought, *let them bury it there. It won't be hard to find.*

Now there was a voice—a very low voice—Injun Joe's: "Curse her, maybe she's got company! There's lights on."

A deadly chill went to Huck's heart—this must be the "revenge job"! His thought was to run away. Then he remembered that the Widow Douglas had been kind to him, and maybe these men were going to murder her. He wished he could go warn her, but he knew he didn't dare.

"Yes. Well, there *is* company there, I reckon. Better forget it, Joe," said the partner.

"Forget it, just when I'm getting out of this country forever? Forget it and maybe never have another chance? I tell you again, I don't care for her money—you may have it. But her husband was rough on me. He was the man that had me horsewhipped—with all the town looking on! *Horsewhipped!*—do you understand? *He's* dead now—but I'll take it out on *her.*"

"Oh, don't kill her! Don't do that!"

"Kill? Who said anything about killing? I would kill *him* if he was here, but not her. When you want to get revenge on a woman you don't kill her—you go for her looks. You cut her face bad!"

"By God, that's awful!"

"If you don't help me with this, I'll kill you. Do you understand that? And if I have to kill you, I'll kill her—and then I reckon nobody will ever know who done this crime."

"Well, if it's got to be done, let's get at it. The quicker the better."

"Do it *now*, while company's there? No—we'll wait till the lights are out."

Huck backed away a few steps as quietly as he could. Then he turned and ran until he reached the Welshman's house. He banged at the door, and the heads of the old man and his two sons popped out of the windows.

"What's going on there? Who's banging? What do you want?" cried the Welshman.

"Let me in—quick! I'll tell everything."

"Why, who are you?"

"Huckleberry Finn—quick, let me in!"

"Huckleberry Finn! It ain't a name to open many doors, but let him in, lads, and let's see what's the trouble."

"Please don't ever tell I told you," were Huck's first words when he got in. "Please don't—I'd be killed, sure—but the Widow Douglas has been good friends to me sometimes, and I want to tell you."

"By George, he has got something to tell, or he wouldn't act so!" cried the old man. "Out with it, and nobody here will ever tell, lad."

Huck told all he had heard, and three minutes later the old man and his sons were up the hill, entering the bushes on tiptoe, their guns in their hands. Huck hid behind a big rock and listened. All of a sudden there was an explosion of guns and a cry.

Huck waited no longer. He jumped up and ran down the hill as fast as his legs could carry him.

CHAPTER FIFTEEN

A Widow is Saved – A Cave is Searched

As soon as the sun came up on Sunday, Huck went back up the hill and rapped at the Welshman's door.

"Who's there?"

"Please let me in! It's only Huck Finn!"

"It's a name that can open this door, night or day—and welcome," said the Welshman. "Now, my boy, I hope you're good and hungry, because breakfast will be ready soon. I and the boys hoped you'd come back here last night."

"I was awful scared," said Huck, "and I ran when the pistols went off. I've come now becuz I wanted to know what happened. Are those devils dead?"

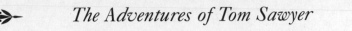

"No, they ain't dead. Just as we sneaked up on them, I sneezed—and they took off running. We fired some shots and they fired back, but we didn't catch them. The Sheriff, his men, and my boys will search the woods this morning. I wish we knew what those rascals looked like. But you couldn't see what they looked like in the dark, could you?"

"Oh, yes. I saw them in town and followed 'em."

"Good! Describe them—describe them, my boy!"

"One's the old deaf and dumb Spaniard that's been hanging around here, and the other's a mean-looking, ragged—"

"That's enough, lad, we know the men! Happened to see them in the woods back of the widow's one day, and they sneaked away. Get going, boys, and tell the Sheriff."

The Welshman's sons left at once. As they were leaving the room, Huck jumped up, shouting:

"Oh, please don't tell anybody it was me that told on them!"

"All right if you say so, Huck, but you ought to get the credit for what you did."

"Oh, no, no! Please don't tell!"

When the young men were gone, the old Welshman said, "They won't tell—and I won't.

But why don't you want it known?"

Huck would not explain, except to say that he would be killed if the men thought he knew anything about them.

"How did you come to follow these men?" asked the Welshman. "Were they acting strange?"

Huck didn't want to tell the whole story, so he said he just happened to wake up around midnight and go out walking, and that he noticed the deaf and dumb Spaniard and his ragged partner, and thought they might be robbers.

"Then they went on," said the Welshman, "and you followed 'em?"

"Followed 'em—yes. That was it. I tracked 'em to the widow's gate and stood in the dark and heard the ragged man beg for the widow's life, and the Spaniard swear he'd spoil her looks just as I told you and your two—"

"What?! The *deaf and dumb* man said all that? How could he talk?"

Huck was caught! He was trying his best to keep the old man from knowing who the Spaniard might be, but he kept making mistakes in his story. The Welshman knew that Huck was not telling him the whole story. He put his hand on Huck's shoulder.

"My boy, don't be afraid of me. This Spaniard is not deaf and dumb. He *can* hear and he *can* talk. You've let that slip out without meaning to, and you can't cover that up now. You know something about that Spaniard that you want to keep hidden. Now, trust me—tell me what it is, and trust ol' Jones— I won't let you get in trouble."

Huck looked into the old man's honest eyes a moment, then bent over and whispered in his ear:

"It ain't a Spaniard—it's Injun Joe!"

Mr. Jones almost jumped out of his chair.

"That sounds exactly like something Injun Joe would do. Now come, my boy, and have something to eat. You look very sickly."

During breakfast the talk went on. Huck didn't say a thing about the treasure. And he was pretty sure the Welshman hadn't found it, because he had said that all he and his boys had come across was a bag of robber's tools. Huck figured that the treasure must still be in Room 2. The men would be caught and jailed, and he and Tom could go get the gold that night.

Just after breakfast, there was a knock at the door. Huck jumped for a hiding place. Several people came in, among them the Widow Douglas. The Welshman told the story to the visitors. The widow went on and on thanking him for his help.

"Don't say a word about it, madam. There's someone else to be thanked more than me, but he don't allow me to tell his name. We wouldn't have been there if it weren't for him."

Everybody at church that morning was talking about the news of the night before. When the sermon was finished, Judge Thatcher's wife walked out with Mrs. Harper.

"Is my Becky going to sleep all day?" she said to Mrs. Harper.

"Your Becky?"

"Yes!" Mrs. Thatcher had a startled look. "Didn't she stay with you last night?"

"Why, no."

Mrs. Thatcher turned pale and sat down, just as Aunt Polly passed by.

"Good morning, Mrs. Thatcher," said Aunt Polly. "Good morning, Mrs. Harper. I've got a boy that's turned up missing. I reckon my Tom stayed at one of your houses last night. And now he's afraid to come to church."

Mrs. Thatcher shook her head sadly and turned whiter than ever.

"He didn't stay with us," said Mrs. Harper, looking upset as her son, Joe, walked over.

"Joe Harper, have you seen my Tom this morning?" Aunt Polly asked worriedly.

"No, ma'am."

"When did you see him last?"

Joe couldn't say for sure. The other children said they didn't remember seeing Tom and Becky get on the ferryboat. It had been dark and nobody had thought much about it. One young man finally said he was afraid that they were still in the cave! Mrs. Thatcher fainted. Aunt Polly began crying.

The alarm went out and the whole village started a search. Soon, two hundred men were heading toward the cave. All night, Mrs. Thatcher, Aunt Polly, and the town waited for news, but when morning dawned all the word that came was: "Send more candles—and send food."

The old Welshman came home toward daylight the next morning, worn out from helping to search the cave. He found Huck still in bed, sick with fever. The doctors were all at the cave, so the Widow Douglas came to stay with Huck.

The search dragged on for three awful days and nights. Men searched the tunnels, calling out for Tom and Becky and firing pistol shots. In a far part of the cave, the words "Becky and Tom" had been found traced upon the rocky wall in candle smoke. Nearby lay a piece of Becky's ribbon. Mrs. Thatcher cried that this would be the last memento of Becky she would ever have.

Huck stayed in a feverish sleep for days. During one wakeful moment he asked the Widow Douglas if Tom had been to see him. The old woman just said, "Hush, child," and began to cry. Huck didn't know what to think of that, but fell back into a deep sleep.

CHAPTER SIXTEEN

Lost! – A Light in the Darkness

Now to return to Tom and Becky and their day at the picnic. They had explored all the side tunnels of the cave, lighting candles as things got darker and darker. Bats squeaked and flew into their faces. Water dripped onto their heads from the top of the cave. Before long, they were squeezing through very narrow tunnels. Tom wanted to show Becky all he knew, or *thought* he knew, about this mysterious world. On one wall they wrote their names using candle smoke. After some time, they came to an underground lake and sat down to rest. Now, for the first time, they realized how still and quiet it was.

"Why, I didn't notice," said Becky, "but it seems a long time since I heard any of the others. I wonder how long we've been down here, Tom. We better start back."

"Yes, I reckon we better."

"Can you find the way, Tom? It's all a mixed-up crookedness to me."

"I reckon I could find it. But let's not go by the bats again. If they put our candles out, it will be an awful mess. Let's try some other way."

They went through a tunnel, but everything looked strange to Tom. He began to think they were lost. Becky clung to his side in fear and started to cry.

Tom began shouting, hoping someone would hear him. The children stood still and listened, but there was no reply. Tom turned back the way they had come, but could not be sure which turns they had taken. Soon Becky knew that Tom could not find his way back.

"Tom, Tom, we're lost! We're lost! We never can get out of this awful place! Oh, why did we ever leave the others?"

She sank to the ground, crying. Tom put his arms around her to comfort her, and they went on again.

Tom blew out Becky's candle. They only had a few left and had to save them. Becky knew what this meant, and she lost hope.

They grew more and more tired until, at last Becky had to sit down. Tom rested with her, and they talked of home and their friends. Becky cried, and Tom tried to think of some way to help her. Before too long, she had fallen asleep.

When Becky woke up, they wandered along some more, hand in hand. A long time after this they came to a spring, and Tom said it was time to rest again. Tom fastened his candle to the wall in front of them with a bit of clay. Nothing was said for some time. Then Becky broke the silence:

"Tom, I am so hungry!"

Tom took a small piece of cake from his pocket, saved from the picnic. They both agreed it could be their "wedding cake." It would give them something to dream about. It tasted so good that Becky wanted to move on again, but Tom looked seriously into her eyes.

"Becky, can you stand it if I tell you something?"

Becky's face went white, but she nodded yes.

"Well… Becky, we must stay here where there's water. That little piece of wax is our last candle!"

"Tom!" Becky sobbed. "Won't they miss us and hunt for us?"

"Yes, they will! Certainly they will!"

"When would they miss us, Tom?"

"When they get back to the boat, I reckon."

"Tom, it might be dark then—would they notice we haven't come back?"

"I don't know. But anyway, your mother will miss you as soon as they get home."

Then they both remembered that Becky's mother had not expected her home that night. It could have been as late as Sunday noon before Mrs. Thatcher found out that Becky was not at Mrs. Harper's house.

The children watched the small bit of candle melt slowly away. The flame grew weaker, and then… everything was total darkness.

Time dragged on. They slept again, and awoke starving and sad. Tom believed it must be Tuesday by this time.

Then he had an idea. There were some side tunnels nearby. It would be better to search than do nothing at all.

He took a kite line from his pocket, tied it to a spot on the cave wall, and he and Becky started out, unwinding the line as they crawled along. At the end of twenty steps he came to what felt like a cliff or a jumping-off place. Tom got down on his knees and felt below and as far around the corner to the right as he could reach. At that moment, not twenty yards away, a human hand, holding a candle, appeared from behind a rock! Tom lifted up a happy shout, but instantly that hand was followed by the body it belonged to—Injun Joe's!

Tom was frozen with fear. He was most happy to see Injun Joe turn and run out of sight. He did not tell Becky what it was he had seen. He told her he had only shouted "for luck."

But fear gave way to hunger. After another long sleep, Tom thought that it must be Wednesday or Thursday or even Friday or Saturday now, and that the search had been given up. He decided to explore another tunnel. He felt willing to risk Injun Joe and all other terrors to find a way out.

But Becky was very weak. She said she would wait where she was, and die. With a lump in his throat, Tom kissed her cheek and tried to act brave. Then he took the kite line in his hand and went crawling down one of the tunnels, full of fear of the unknown.

Tuesday evening came, and the village of St. Petersburg still cried for its lost children. Most of the searchers had given up. The village went to bed on Tuesday night feeling hopeless.

Sometime in the middle of the night, village church bells began ringing. In a moment the streets were filled with people shouting, "They're found!

They're found!" Tin pans rang and horns blew as the people marched together toward the river. At last they were met by the children being drawn in a carriage. The villagers shouted hurrah after hurrah! It was the greatest night the little town had ever seen.

Tom lay on a sofa, telling the story of the wonderful adventure (adding a few extra things to make it more exciting). He told of how he left Becky to find a way out of the cave, following two paths as far as his kite line would reach. And how he followed a third and was about to turn back when he spotted a far-off speck of daylight. He told how he dropped the line, pushed his head and shoulders through a small hole, and saw the broad Mississippi River rolling by! He was proud to say that he had comforted Becky and kept her from dying, and had helped her find her way out. Then he told of how some men came along, gave them some food, and brought them home.

Three days and nights of hunger in the cave had been hard on Tom and Becky. They stayed in bed all day Wednesday and all of Thursday.

Tom got around town a little by Friday, but Becky did not leave her room until Sunday.

Tom learned of Huck's sickness, but was not allowed to see him until Monday. He saw Huck each day at the widow's house after that, but was warned to keep still about  his adventure in the cave and to say nothing that would excite Huck. At home, Tom learned what had happened on Cardiff Hill and also that Injun Joe's partner had been found dead in the river, near the ferrylanding. It was thought he had drowned while trying to escape.

About two weeks after Tom's rescue from the cave, he started off one morning to visit Huck, who was now strong enough to hear exciting talk—and Tom thought he had some that would interest him. Judge Thatcher's house was on Tom's way, so he stopped to see Becky. While he was there, he told Judge Thatcher that he wouldn't mind going back into the cave.

"Well, there are others just like you, I'm sure," said the Judge. "But we have taken care of that. Nobody will ever get lost in that cave again."

"Why?" asked Tom.

"Because I had its big door shut and sealed with iron and triple-locks—and I've got the keys."

Tom turned as white as a sheet.

"What's the matter, boy? Out with it! What is it?"

"Oh, Judge, Injun Joe's in the cave!"

CHAPTER SEVENTEEN

Return to the Cave – Under the Cross

Within a few minutes the news had spread, and boatloads of men were on their way to the cave. Tom Sawyer was in a boat with Judge Thatcher.

The cave door was unlocked and opened to a terrible sight! Injun Joe lay stretched upon the ground, dead. His face was close to the crack of the door and his Bowie knife was in his hand.

Tom felt sorry for him, for he knew how the man must have suffered. But Tom also felt a great relief, for he no longer had live in fear of this man.

Injun Joe was buried near the mouth of the cave. The villagers decided they were as happy with the funeral as they would have been with a hanging.

The morning after the funeral, Tom and Huck had a private talk. Huck had learned all about Tom's adventure from the Welshman and the Widow Douglas, but Tom told him there was one thing he *didn't* know. Before Tom could begin, Huck told about following Injun Joe on the night of the picnic.

"You followed him?" said Tom.

"Yes. If it hadn't been for me he'd be down in Texas by now."

Then Huck told *his* whole story in secret to Tom, who had only heard the Welshman's part of it before.

"And," said Huck, "I found out that Injun Joe wasn't carryin' the treasure that night. So, by now, somebody's sure searched that room and found the money. Anyways, I reckon we're out of luck, Tom. We'll never see that gold."

"Huck, that money wasn't ever in that Room Number Two!"

"What?! Tom, have you got on the track of that money again?"

"Huck, it's in the cave!"

Huck's eyes blazed.

"Say it again, Tom."

"The money's in the cave—it never was in the room in the tavern. That was just a place where Injun Joe went to find some whiskey. It was just plain, dumb luck that we happened to search for him there, thinking we should look for a room number. The *cave* was den Number Two all along."

"Tom—honest now—are you kiddin' me?"

"Honest, Huck—just as honest as ever I was in my life. Will you go in there with me and help get the money out?"

"You bet I will! I will if it's where we can find our way to it and not get lost."

"Huck, we can do that without the least little bit of trouble in the world."

"Good enough! What makes you think the money's—"

"Huck, you just wait till we get in there. If we don't find it, I'll agree to give you my drum and everything I've got in the world, by golly."

"All right—it's a deal. When do we go?"

"Right now, if you're strong enough."

"Is it far in the cave? I can't walk more'n a mile, Tom."

"It's about five mile into there the way anybody but me would go, Huck, but I know a shortcut. I'll take you right to it in a boat."

"Let's start right off, Tom."

"All right. We need some food, and a bag or two, and two or three kite strings, and some matches."

A little after noon, the boys "borrowed" a small boat from someone who was not at home. Several miles below Cave Hollow, Tom pointed out a white place on the hill that he had memorized as a landmark, and the boys went ashore.

"Now, Huck, where we're standing you could touch with a fishing pole that hole I got out of. See if you can find it."

Huck searched all over and found nothing. Tom proudly marched into a thick clump of bushes.

"Here you are! Look at it, Huck. It's the snuggest hole in the county. You just keep mum about it, though. This'll be the perfect place for us when we become robbers! We'll let Joe Harper and Ben Rogers in—because of course there's got to be a gang, or else there wouldn't be any style about it. Tom Sawyer's Gang—it sounds splendid, don't it, Huck?"

"Why, it's real bully, Tom. I believe it's better'n bein' a pirate."

The boys entered the hole, tying kite strings as they went so they could find their way back out. They passed the spring and went on until they reached the "jumping-off place." The candles showed that it was not really a cliff, but only a steep clay hill twenty or thirty feet high.

Tom whispered, "Now I'll show you something, Huck."

Holding his candle up, he said, "Look as far around the corner as you can. Do you see that mark over there on that big rock?"

"Tom, it's a *cross!*"

"*Now* where's your den Number Two? *'Under the cross,'* hey? Right there's where I saw Injun Joe holdin' up his candle, Huck!"

The boys hunted all over. They found some food scraps and blankets that must have been Injun Joe's, but there was no money box.

Finally, they decided it must be under the large rock that had the sign of the cross. Tom began digging under the rock with his knife and soon struck wood.

"Hey, Huck!—you hear that?"

Huck began to dig and scratch now. Some boards were uncovered and removed. Beneath the boards was a small tunnel under the rock. The boys slid into it, holding their candles to light the way. All at once Tom stopped.

"My goodness, Huck, lookyhere!"

It was the treasure box! Along with it were a couple of knives, a belt, and two or three pairs of old moccasins.

"Got it at last!" said Huck, running his hands through the gold coins. "My, but we're rich, Tom!"

"Huck, I always reckoned we'd get it. It's just too good to believe, but we *have* got it, sure! Say— let's not fool around here. Let's snake it out. Lemme see if I can lift the box."

Tom could lift the box but couldn't carry it.

"I thought so," he said. "I reckon I was right to bring the bags along."

The money was soon in the bags, and before long the boys were back in the boat eating their lunch. As the sun began to set, they pushed off and landed just after dark.

"Now, Huck," said Tom, "we'll hide the money in the room above the widow's woodshed. I'll come up in the morning and we'll count it and split it between us, and then we'll hunt up a place out in the woods for it where it will be safe. Just you lay quiet here and watch the stuff till I run and get Benny Taylor's little wagon."

When Tom returned with the wagon, the boys put the two sacks into it, threw some old rags on top, and started off. As they were passing the Welshman's house, Mr. Jones stepped out of the door and said, "Hallo, who's that?"

"Huck! And Tom Sawyer."

"Good! Come along with me, boys. You are keeping everybody waiting. Here, I'll haul the wagon for you. Why, it's pretty heavy. Got bricks in it?—or old metal?"

"Old metal," said Tom, thinking quickly.

"I thought so. The boys in this town will take more trouble and fool away more time hunting a little old iron to sell. But—hurry along inside, now!"

Soon Huck and Tom found themselves in Mrs. Douglas's parlor. Mr. Jones left the wagon near the door and followed them in. The place was all lit up, and there stood Tom's family and all the important people of the village, dressed in fancy clothes.

"Tom wasn't at home yet, so I gave him up," said the Welshman. "But I stumbled on him and Huck right at my door, and so I just brought them along in a hurry."

"And you did just right," said the widow. "Come with me, boys."

She took them to a bedroom and said, "Now wash and dress yourselves. Here are two new suits of clothes—shirts, socks, everything complete. Get into them and come down when you're cleaned up enough." Then she left.

CHAPTER EIGHTEEN

Riches – Rules – Rags – Robbers

Huck said, "Tom, we can slide out of here if we can find a rope. The window ain't high up."

"Shucks! What do you want to run away for?"

"Well, I ain't used to that kind of a crowd. I can't stand it. I ain't going down there, Tom."

"Oh, bother! It ain't anything. I don't mind it a bit. I'll take care of you."

Some minutes later, the widow's guests were at the supper table. Mr. Jones made a short speech, in which he thanked the widow for having the dinner honoring him and his two sons for protecting her. Then he sprung the secret about how Huck had been the *real* hero in helping to save the widow.

The widow showed her surprise at this and piled thanks after thanks on Huck, who was mighty uncomfortable being the center of attention.

The widow said she was going to give Huck a home under her roof and send him to school, and that when she could spare the money, she would start him in business. Tom saw his chance and spoke up:

"Huck don't need it. Huck's rich. Huck's got money. Oh, you needn't smile—I reckon I can show you. You just wait a minute."

Tom ran out the door. The company looked at each other and at Huck, who was too tongue-tied to speak. Tom returned with the sacks, and poured all the coins on the table.

"There," he said. "Half of it's Huck's, and half of it's mine!"

Everyone was shocked and speechless for a minute. Then they all wanted an explanation. Tom said he could give it, and told the whole story.

The money was counted, and the sum came to over twelve thousand dollars. It was more cash than anyone there had ever seen at one time before.

The boys' money was the talk of St. Petersburg. Everyone began to say nice things about Huck and Tom. The village paper even printed stories about them.

The Widow Douglas put Huck's money in the bank to earn six percent interest, and Judge Thatcher did the same with Tom's, at Aunt Polly's request. Each boy had all the money he needed—a dollar a day from the interest!

Judge Thatcher came to think a lot of Tom. He said that no common boy would ever have got his daughter out of the cave, and that he hoped to see Tom become a great lawyer or a great soldier some day.

Because Huck Finn was now rich and under the Widow Douglas's care, he was dragged into society—and his pain was almost more than he could stand. The widow's servants kept him clean and neat, and they made him sleep in clean white sheets. He had to eat with a knife and fork and use a napkin, cup, and plate. He had to learn his books and go to church. And he had to speak just right.

He put up with this new way of life for three weeks, and then ran away.

Early one morning, after Huck had been missing for three days, Tom Sawyer found Huck just where he thought he would—in among some large, empty barrels. He was dirty, messy, and dressed in his old rags. Tom told him the trouble his disappearance had been causing, and begged him to go home. Huck's face looked sad.

"Don't talk about it, Tom. I've tried it, and it don't work. Tom, it ain't for me. I ain't used to it. The widow is good to me, and friendly, but I can't stand them ways. She makes me wash, and they comb me all to thunder. I got to wear them awful clothes, and go to church. I can't spit. I got to wear shoes all Sunday. I can't take it any more, Tom."

"Well, everybody does that way, Huck."

"Tom, I ain't everybody, and I can't *stand* it. It's awful to be tied up so. I got to ask to go a-fishing. I got to ask to go in a-swimming. Widow Douglas wouldn't let me yell, nor scratch in front of people. And besides that, school's going to open, and I'd-a had to go to it. Lookyhere, Tom, bein' rich ain't what it's cracked up to be. I wouldn't ever got into all this trouble if it hadn't-a been for that money. Now you just take my share of it and gimme a dime sometimes—not many times, becuz I don't give a dern for a thing unless it's hard to git—and you go tell the widow and get me out of this mess."

"Oh, Huck, you know I can't do that. 'Tain't fair. And besides, if you'll try this thing just a while longer, you'll come to like it."

"Like it! Yes—the way I'd like a hot stove if I was to set on it long enough. No, Tom, I like the

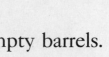

woods and the river and sleepin' in empty barrels. Dern it all! Just as we'd found a secret hideout in a cave and could've become robbers, this foolishness has got to come up and spoil it all!"

Tom saw his chance. "Lookyhere, Huck, being rich ain't going to keep *me* from turning robber."

"No! Are you bein' honest, Tom?"

"Just as dead honest as I'm sitting here. But, Huck, we can't let you into the gang if you ain't respectable, you know."

Huck's joy left him. "Can't let me in, Tom? Didn't you let me be a pirate?"

"Yes, but that's different. A robber is more high-class than what a pirate is—usually."

"Now, Tom, hain't you always been friendly to me? You wouldn't leave me out, *would* you, Tom?"

"Huck, I wouldn't want to, and I *don't* want to—but what would people say? Why, they'd say Tom Sawyer's Gang had pretty low characters in it! They'd mean *you*, Huck. You wouldn't like that, and I wouldn't."

Huck was silent for some time. Finally he said, "Well, I'll go back to Widow Douglas for a month and see if I can learn to stand it, if you'll let me b'long to the gang, Tom."

"All right, Huck, it's a deal! Come along, and I'll ask the widow to let up on you a little."

"Will you, Tom—now, will you? When you going to start the gang and turn robbers?"

"Oh, right away. We'll get the boys together and have the swearing-in tonight, maybe."

"Have the which?"

"The swearing-in."

"What's that?"

"It's to swear to stand by one another, and never tell the gang's secrets, even if you're chopped all to bits."

"That sounds great, Tom, I tell you!"

"Well, I bet it is. And all that swearing's got to be done at midnight, in the lonesomest, awfulest place you can find—a haunted house is the best."

"Well, midnight's good, anyway, Tom."

"Yes, so it is. And you've got to swear on a coffin, and sign it with blood."

"Now, that's the life! Why, it's a million times better than pirating. I'll stick to the widow till I rot, Tom, and if I git to be a reg'lar ripper of a robber, with everybody talking 'bout it, I reckon she'll be proud she snaked me in out of the wet."

THE END

Conclusion

So ends this story. It being a history of a boy, it must stop here. The story could not go much further without becoming the history of a man. When one writes a novel about grown people, he knows exactly where to stop—that is, with a marriage. But when he writes of youngsters, he must stop where he best can.

Most of the characters that perform in this book are still living, and they are happy. Some day it may seem worthwhile to take up the story of the younger ones again and see what sort of men and women they turned out to be. Therefore, it will be wisest not to reveal any of that part of their lives at present.

The Adventures of
Huckleberry Finn

MARK TWAIN

CONDENSED AND RETOLD BY
CLAY STAFFORD

ILLUSTRATED BY
RUTH PALMER

CONTENTS

HUCKLEBERRY FINN — a boy who'd rather think for himself (and not be civilized)

TOM SAWYER — Huck Finn's best buddy

WIDOW DOUGLAS — the rich old lady who takes Huck in

MISS WATSON — the widow's sister who wants to civilize Huck

JIM — Miss Watson's slave who runs away to be free

BEN ROGERS, JOE HARPER, TOMMY BARNES — some of Tom and Huck's buddies

JUDGE THATCHER — a good man who keeps Huck's $6,000 safe for him

PAP — Huck's mean ol' dad who wants Huck's $6,000

SARAH MARY WILLIAMS/GEORGE PETERS — a girl… no, a boy… no, Huck Finn in disguise

THE DUKE — the younger of the two "actors" who meet up with Huck and Jim

THE KING — the older of the two "actors" who lie, cheat, and steal

MARY JANE, SUSAN AND JOANNA — the three daughters of Peter Wilks, who has died

HARVEY AND WILLIAM WILKS — the English Uncles of the three girls… but not really…

HARVEY AND WILLIAM WILKS — the English Uncles of the three girls… really…

DOCTOR ROBINSON — the only one who sees through the fraud

LEVI BELL — a lawyer with a good idea

UNCLE SILAS PHELPS — Huck's new "Uncle," Tom's real uncle, Jim's captor

AUNT SALLY — Huck's new "Aunt," Tom's real aunt

TOM SAWYER — Huck's new name, Tom's real name

SID SAWYER — Tom's brother, played by Tom himself, because Huck is Tom… Aw, read the book!

NAT — a slave who takes food to a locked-up runaway (Jim!)

NOTICE

This tale has no reason,
No lesson can be found.
If you want a moral,
Quick! Put this story down!

By Order of the Author

The Adventures of
Huckleberry Finn

CHAPTER ONE

Huck is Civilized – Tom's Gang – Fishhooks

Unless you've read *The Adventures of Tom Sawyer* (which I hope you have), you don't know me. That book ended with Tom Sawyer and me finding hidden money in a cave. Because we found it, Judge Thatcher let us keep it. He put it in a bank for us, and we got a dollar a day. By anybody's standards, we were rich.

I've taken care of myself most of my life— though I'm still a kid. I wore what I wanted, slept where I wanted. After I became rich, a woman named Widow Douglas adopted me. She said she was going to "civilize" me. She dressed me up in

fancy clothes that itched and made me sweat. I ran away once, but Tom Sawyer found me and talked me into coming back.

Widow Douglas had rules aplenty. You had to come when she rang a bell, learn about dead people in the Bible, say prayers over food, sit straight, stand straight, and not smoke (even though she dipped snuff). I put up with it until Widow Douglas's sister, Miss Watson, came to live with us. She tried to teach me to read. I told her "no thanks." She told me I'd go to the Bad Place. I told her that would be fine by me. Since she had said earlier that Tom Sawyer would be there, I figured I'd be in good company.

After that lecture, I stole upstairs and sat by the window. (Owls hooted about someone who *had* died. Dogs and whippoorwills told about people *going* to die.) I flipped a spider off me. It dropped in the candle wax and shriveled up before I could get it out. Something bad was about to happen. Miss Watson and Widow Douglas snored down the hall. The clock in the town square struck twelve. I heard a twig snap.

"Me-yow! Me-yow!" came out of the darkness.

I smiled.

I called back like a cat, blew out the candle, climbed out the window onto the shed roof, and jumped to the ground. Tom Sawyer waited for me behind a tree.

— —

Miss Watson was very prim and proper, but she still owned a slave. His name was Jim. They didn't let him come in the house so he had to sleep on the porch. (I bet he didn't have to learn to read either.)

Just as Tom and I snuck by Jim, I tripped on a root and made a noise.

"Who's there?" Jim asked as he woke up.

Tom and I dropped to the ground.

Jim came down the steps and stood right beside us. After about five minutes he said, "I'll just sit down here until I hear that noise again. Then I'll catch you." Lord if he didn't sit right between Tom and me and almost hit me in the face with his foot. His sitting didn't last long, though, because soon he started snoring. Tom gave me the signal to follow.

We crept down to the river and met Ben Rogers, Joe Harper, and a few other waiting boys. We unhitched a small flat-bottom boat and, using a pole, piloted it down the river to a rocky bluff. As we climbed ashore, we had no idea where Tom intended to take us. We finally stopped hiking at a clump of bushes. Tom made us swear to keep everything a secret. We all agreed. Tom ordered Joe Harper to light the candles. We then got down on our hands and knees and crawled into a hole that led into a huge underground cave.

"We're going to be a band of robbers," Tom said. He always said we would be something. This time it was robbers. "Anyone who wants to join Tom Sawyer's Gang must sign his name in blood."

We all agreed heartily.

Tom took out a piece of paper. After we pricked our fingers with a pin and made our marks on Tom's paper, Ben Rogers asked, "What does this club do, anyway?"

"Robbery," Tom said.

"You mean like stealing cattle or robbing houses?"

"That's not robbery," Tom said. "That's burglary. We're robbers. We rob stagecoaches. We might even ransom somebody."

"What's ransom?"

"Who knows," Tom said. "It's just done."

"Look at Little Tommy Barnes!" Joe Harper exclaimed.

Tommy had fallen asleep. Ben waked him up with a pinch. Tommy started crying.

"That's no way to be a robber," Joe said.

"I don't want to be a robber anymore," Tommy said back. Everybody made fun of him until Tommy said he would tell all of our secrets. Tom gave him five cents to be quiet. Tommy agreed to the silence.

We argued over when we should begin robbing. Some said Sunday, but it seemed rather wicked to begin a life of robbery on the holy day. We finally decided that next week we would get together sometime to determine when we would get together.

Ben Rogers called elections because every club needs officers. We all elected Tom Sawyer as first captain and Joe Harper as second captain.

That's how we began.

When I finally got back to the Widow Douglas's, the sun had just come up. I didn't bother taking off my filthy clothes before I went to sleep.

At breakfast, Miss Watson scolded me because of my clothes. Widow Douglas kept quiet. Because the Widow didn't fuss, I thought I'd try to be nice, but changed my mind when Miss Watson insisted I get in the closet and pray.

"God answers prayers," she said.

It made me glad to hear it. She said I should pray to learn to obey. I prayed for fishhooks, which seemed to me more useful. When none appeared, I told Miss Watson through the closet door that praying didn't seem to work. She called me a fool.

I never did get those fishhooks.

CHAPTER TWO

Boot Prints–Dear Ol' Pap–The Cabin

School started, winter came, and I learned to read a few words and do a little math. On warm nights, I still snuck out and slept in the woods. I liked the old ways, but on cold nights I began to like the new ways, too.

One morning I spilled the salt at breakfast (which is bad luck). Before I could throw a pinch over my shoulder (for good luck), Miss Watson caught me. I left the house walking kind of slow, wondering when bad luck would happen. At the garden gate I saw a man's tracks in an inch of fresh snow. I recognized the boot print. I ran to Judge Thatcher's.

"I guess you've come for some of your money," the Judge said.

"No," I replied. "I don't even want to *own* my money. I want to *give* it to you."

"Give it to me? Oho-o! I see. You mean you want to *sell* me your property?"

"Yes," I said. "Don't ask me why and I won't tell you lies."

Being a judge, Judge Thatcher happily wrote up a paper that, he said, sold my $6,000 to him for $1 to make it legal. It didn't seem like the best deal, but the judge assured me it was the best way to go.

I found Jim. He had a hairball that told people's fortunes. I told Jim I saw my Pap's tracks in the snow even though everybody told me my Pap had died. Jim said something over his hairball and dropped it. It rolled a little. Jim got down on the ground and put his ear against it.

"It won't talk without money," Jim said.

I didn't tell Jim about the dollar I had in my pocket, but gave him a fake quarter instead. Suddenly, Jim heard the hairball speak.

"Your Pap is in town," Jim said. "He's got one good angel sitting on one shoulder and a bad

angel sitting on the other. What he does next depends on which angel he listens to."

I left Jim on the front porch, lit my candle, and went upstairs to my room.

*   *   *

I shut the door. When I turned around, there was my dead Pap—sitting in a chair, very much alive. I gasped.

"Fancy clothes, boy. You think you're pretty sharp, don't you?"

"Maybe I do, maybe I don't."

"Don't get smart with me, boy."

His oily black hair and whiskers dangled. His skin glowed white in the candlelight like a dead man's. His clothes smelled like pig slop and hung in rags.

"I hear you've learned to read and write."

"Yep."

"Well, stop it. Your dead momma never learned to read. I ain't learned to read. You ain't going to. What's this?" He held up a drawing.

"That's a picture the teacher gave me for doing my lessons."

He tore it up. "Ain't no more. I hear you're rich."

"I ain't."

"Judge Thatcher's got your money, I heard."

"I don't have any money. Ask Judge Thatcher."

"I'll do that. How much money you got on you?"

"A dollar. But I'm…"

"Give it to me."

I gave it to him because I knew if I didn't he'd beat me. Pap left—and left me wondering what he'd do next.

Pap tried to get my money, but Judge Thatcher wouldn't give it to him. Pap said he'd take Judge Thatcher to court. He started hanging around Widow Douglas's and he treated me pretty bad when he caught a-hold of me. The Widow told him to leave—so he did, but he stole *me* with him! He put me on a flat-bottom boat, took me three miles up the river, and locked me in a cabin. He had a gun, so I couldn't get away.

Two months passed and then Pap disappeared for three days. I thought he'd been killed or drowned. I worried I'd die locked in

the cabin. I found an old saw blade and used it to try to cut my way out. Before I could finish, I heard Pap coming.

He'd been to get supplies. He said his lawsuit against Judge Thatcher had almost reached the court. His lawyer said when it did Pap would get the money. He also said the Widow Douglas had sued for custody of me, and this time she might win. That meant I'd have to go back to reading.

"I'd like to see the Widow try to get you," he said. "I've got a place up in the woods where no one would ever find you."

That thought scared me more than reading. What if he locked me up somewhere and never came back? I decided that during the night I'd try to escape from him *and* the Widow Douglas! Neither life suited me at the moment.

Pap started drinking while I cooked supper. "A widow's got no right to steal a man's son and try to make the son better than the daddy," he said.

Finally, Pap got so drunk he fell onto the bed. While I waited for him to go to sleep, I accidentally fell asleep myself.

"Get up!" Pap said the next morning.

"Huh?" I asked.

"Did somebody try to break into the cabin?" he asked.

"No." I figured he'd seen where I tried to break out.

Pap looked at me kind of funny. Then his head nodded, letting me know his brain finally caught up. "Go see if there's any fish for breakfast."

It delighted me to leave the cabin. As I walked the riverbank, I saw an empty canoe drifting down the river. I jumped into the river and brought it ashore. Pap would be happy to have it. As I climbed on the bank, though, another thought hit me. *When I ran away, instead of running on foot, I could take the canoe.* I hid it well in the vines.

I met Pap on the path. He whopped me up the side of my head for not checking all the fish lines. I told him I fell in the river and it took some time to get back out. He believed me. We caught five catfish that morning.

After breakfast, Pap said, "I need to go back into town. We need more bacon."

Pap locked me in the cabin and I finished sawing out the hole. Then I fixed the hole back so he would not know what I'd done. I went outside to the front of the cabin, took an ax and chopped down the door. Next I squished some boxbog berries in a cup. They looked just like blood. (Most people can't tell the difference.) I smeared the boxbog "blood" all over the cabin. I wanted Pap to think someone had attacked me.

I had another idea. I took a sack of flour, cut a hole in it, and left a trail of flour from the cabin into the woods. Pap would think a thief killed me and stole the flour—and his hunting gun!

I grabbed the gun, some supplies and food, and hurried back to the canoe to wait for the moon to rise.

Night came. Pap came up the river just as I got ready to go. I hid the canoe back in the vines. When he disappeared towards the cabin, I paddled off from the Missouri shore. I stopped several miles downriver at Jackson's Island.

I thought no one would find me there.

CHAPTER THREE

Finding Jim –
Our Island – The Floating House

I awoke that morning to a BOOM! I saw a ferryboat out on the river that was firing a cannon. I could see Pap, Judge Thatcher, Tom Sawyer, and several others on board. The cannon "boom" was supposed to raise a dead body in the river. They were looking for me!

They shot the cannon again, and straight towards me! I was deaf from the blast, blind from the smoke, and expected my spirit to rise from my body at any minute. They didn't see me.

I built a campfire that night and lived lazily, eating food I had taken from the cabin and adding berries I found in the woods. After about a week, I decided to explore the island. Then I smelled something. I hurried through the brush and before I knew it I came upon an open space where a fresh campfire still smoked. I jumped back into the underbrush and half-crawled back to my canoe. I loaded everything in and hid.

By night, I had gotten mighty hungry. I knew I couldn't start a fire on the island if someone else was living on it as well. So I got in the canoe and paddled over to the Illinois side of the river. I'd just finished a hot meal when I heard horses coming. I put out my fire.

"It's getting late," I heard a man say. "The horses are tired. Let's camp. We'll find him tomorrow."

I paddled back to the island, thinking they were searching for me. I tried to sleep but couldn't, knowing someone might be on the island. In the dark, I got Pap's gun and began slinking through the woods. Just at daybreak, I came to the place where I'd found the fire. Lo and behold!

"Hey, Jim!" I said coming out of the bushes.

Miss Watson's slave jumped to his feet.

"Don't hurt me!" he yelled. "I never done anything bad to dead people!"

I told him, "I'm not dead." He finally believed me after poking me in the stomach. "Make up the campfire," I said. "Let's eat breakfast." It made me so happy not to be lonely anymore.

"What's the use when all you've got is berries?" Jim asked.

"Berries?" I asked.

"That's all I've eaten since I've been on the island, ever since you were killed."

I took Jim back to the canoe and showed him all my supplies.

"I feel like I've died and gone to Heaven," he said.

After breakfast we talked. I told him about how I'd squished the boxbog berries and made it look like my blood. Jim was impressed. He told me, "Tom Sawyer himself couldn't have come up with anything that smart."

I asked Jim what he was doing on the island.

"Better not tell," he said.

"Why?"

"There's reasons. If I told you, you wouldn't tell on me, would you?"

"No," I said.

"I ran off."

I couldn't believe it. I'd been taught it was wrong for a slave to run away. But I had given him my word, just as I would any man, and I wasn't about to go back on him. Jim told me he heard Miss Watson planned to sell him to a man in New Orleans for $800. I couldn't believe it.

"Miss Watson's mean, honey," he said.

"She's been mean to me, too," I said. "At least she didn't make you read."

"I would have liked if she did," he said.

That surprised me, but I quickly forgot about it as Jim told me how he had escaped.

"When they left to look for your body," Jim told me, "I took my chance. With the river high, logs floated by on a regular basis. I took one headed here. That log ride made me a rich man. I hear I'm worth $800." He smiled as he said it.

～ ～ ～

Our island was only three miles long and a quarter of a mile deep. I wanted to explore an area I'd seen earlier in the middle of the island.

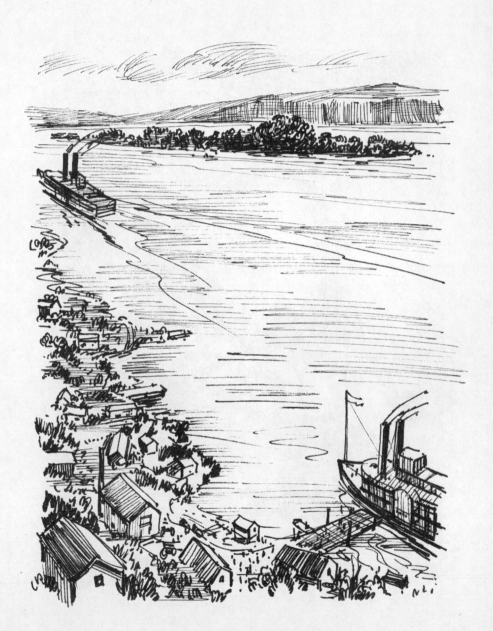

The area was a rocky ridge, thick with bushes and steep faces. Almost to the top, we found a cavern inside the rock about as large as three rooms in a regular house. Jim could stand in it without having to stoop.

"Let's bring our things up here," Jim said.

"I don't want to climb this everyday," I said.

"We could hide here. No one could find us without dogs. And there's signs in the air it's going to rain tonight."

I finally agreed.

We got the supplies from the canoe. By the time we finished, it was dinner time. We cooked at the edge of the cave and had our blankets spread inside. The skies opened up and the rain fell. Darkness came. Thunder and lightning. We watched it from the dry room of our little cavern.

"Jim, I like this better than anywhere. Pass me more cornbread and fish, would you?"

"If you hadn't listened to me, you'd be down there, child," he pointed. "Hungry. Soaking wet."

I also might have been drowned.

The river rose so high that, during the next day, Jim and I paddled around on the island in our canoe! Rabbits, snakes, and anything that had to breathe air hunkered on tree limbs and logs to stay out of the flow.

The island stayed flooded for several days. Only at night did we allow ourselves to go away from the island where someone might see us.

One night, while drifting in the river, we found a plank lumber raft—nine boards worth. We brought it to the island.

Another night a two-story house floated by. Jim thought we should climb aboard. Inside, Jim found a man, dead for several days. Somebody had shot him in the back. I wanted to see the dead man, but Jim wouldn't let me look.

We found all sorts of clothes and things in the house that we might need later. We loaded everything into the canoe.

By the time we started back, we had floated a quarter mile below the island. Daylight came upon us. I told Jim to lie down in the canoe and cover himself, 'cause I didn't want him getting caught as I paddled to the island.

As far as I know, no one saw us.

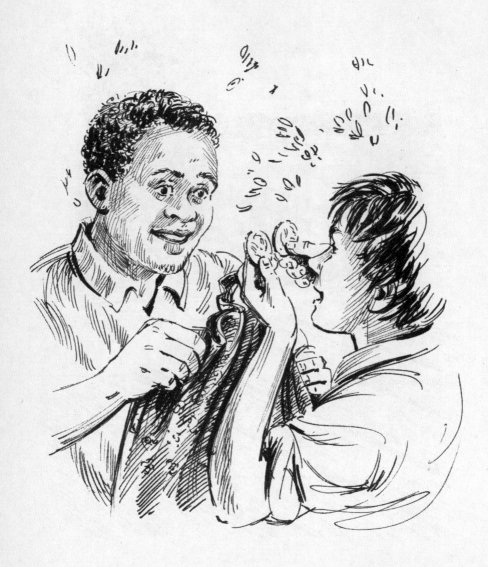

We found eight dollar coins sewn in some of the dresses we took from the floating house.

"I think these clothes were stolen," Jim said.

"How do you figure?" I asked.

"If someone knew the money was sewn into the hems, would they have left the money behind? Whoever had these clothes last didn't know the money was there."

"They musta killed that man, too," I said.

"It's bad luck to talk about the dead," Jim said.

"Bad luck? If this is bad luck, I'd like more of it." I held up eight dollars.

"Bad luck's coming, child," said Jim.

Days passed and boredom set in. I wanted to go to town. We decided to dress me as a girl using the clothes we'd found in the floating house. A bonnet would hide my face.

When dark came, I paddled to shore. The current drifted me below the town, in front of a little shanty. Through the window, I saw a woman. I didn't know her, so I figured she shouldn't know me. I decided she could tell me the latest news about my death and Jim's disappearance. I knocked on the door.

CHAPTER FOUR

Disguise – The Wreck – Kings and Frenchmen

"Come in here," the woman said. "What's your name?"

"Sarah Williams," I said.

I told her I traveled by foot from Hookerville, seven miles south. "My mother's sick. I'm hoping my Uncle Abner Moore will help us."

"I don't know Mr. Moore. My husband will travel with you when he returns. We've only lived here two weeks. Times are tough."

"Yes, ma'am."

"It would be nice to collect that reward money," she said.

"What money?"

"Don't you know? The town has offered three hundred dollars for a runaway slave, and two hundred dollars for old man Finn. Folks suspect one of them may have murdered that boy. You've heard about the murder?"

"Yes, ma'am," I said. "Awful."

"Some thinks the runaway slave killed that poor Huck Finn. Others think his own father did it."

I couldn't tell her differently. I worried for Jim.

"The reward money should bring both of them in," she said. "Old Man Finn has probably left the country, but the black man may be hiding around here somewhere. I talked with the neighbors next door and asked them if anybody lived on Jackson's Island."

I stiffened up.

"They said 'No.' I didn't tell them I saw smoke from a campfire burning over there yesterday. For three hundred dollars, I thought to myself, it's worth checking out. My husband and another man are going over there tonight. If they find the runaway, we'll split the money, and the black man will be hanged for the murder of Huck Finn."

I started squirming. I had to get to Jim.

"What did you call yourself?" she asked.

I couldn't remember what I had told her. "Mary."

"I thought you came by the name of Sarah."

"I do," I said. "Sarah Mary Williams."

A rat stuck its head out of a hole in the wall. The woman threw a piece of lead at it, but missed it terribly. "Can you throw? You try for the next one." She fetched the lead and dropped it in my lap. I closed my legs to catch it. "Now, what's your *real* name?" she asked.

"Huh?" Another rat stuck his head out. I threw the lead. If it hadn't jerked its head back, that would have been one sick rat.

"Is it Bill? Or Tom?"

To busy myself, I picked up a needle and thread from the table. "I'm not the prettiest girl..." I said, (I tried to thread the needle, but I shook so badly I kept missing.) "...but you shouldn't make fun of me. I must go."

"You tell me who you are. Are you a runaway?"

"Yes, ma'am," I said. "My name's George Peters. My mother and father both died. The law sent me to a farmer who mistreats me. I couldn't take it anymore, so I dressed in his daughter's clothes and ran away. Please don't send me back."

"Certainly not," she said. "When a cow gets up, which end gets up first?"

"The rear."

"A horse?"

"The front," I said.

"What side of a tree does moss grow on?"

"The north."

"If ten cows graze on a hillside, how many face one direction?"

"They all face the same way."

"You *are* a farm boy," she said. "I thought I might catch you in another lie."

"No, ma'am."

"Well, George, you might fool men with this outfit, but not women. When you thread a needle, hold the needle steady and push the thread through. Don't hold the thread steady and then move the needle. When you throw something, throw it from over your head and miss terribly. And when a girl tries to catch something in her lap, she doesn't clap her legs together like she's wearing pants. Remember those things."

I thanked her and hurried back to the island.

I built a fire. Jim and I loaded the canoe, tied it to the raft we'd hid, and slipped quickly from the island in the darkness as quietly as we could. We saw no one.

By one o'clock, we had sailed the raft below the island. If a boat came by, we agreed to leave the raft and take the canoe towards shore. We forgot to bring the hunting gun, a fishing line, or anything to eat. I did remember the eight dollars.

When daylight came, we hid on the bank. We cut cottonwood trunks and covered the raft to conceal it. When dark came, Jim made a hut on the raft out of some of the planks to keep us cool in the sun and dry in the rain. We also made an extra steering oar in case we lost the one we had.

We traveled the next four nights and hid during the days. The towns glowed pretty in the night; their lights reflected in twinkles in the slow water. Each night I'd stop at one of the towns and buy fifteen cents worth of meal, bacon, or something else to eat. Mornings before

daylight I'd slip into the fields and "borrow" watermelons, pumpkins, or corn. Pap said it didn't count as stealing as long as you planned on returning what you took. Widow Douglas said stealing equaled stealing no matter what you called it. I'm sure they both had a *little bit* of truth, so we only took a *little bit* of what we saw.

The fifth night we drifted below St. Louis, Missouri. The lightning and thunder played out something awful.

That night we found a wrecked steamboat. On board we found all sorts of things including boots, blankets, clothes, books, a spyglass, three boxes of cigars—all kinds of useful things. We'd never been so rich.

I picked up a book and started reading to Jim. It made me glad to know how to read. We couldn't move around during the day. Reading about kings, dukes, earls and such passed the time.

"I didn't realize so many kings lived and breathed," Jim said.

"Of course." I read to him about Louis the Sixteenth.

"Why do they talk so funny?" asked Jim.

"They don't talk like us," I said. "For example, what would you do if someone came up to you and said '*Potty-yous, Frankie*'?"

"If somebody said that to me, I'd hit him over the head for calling me such."

"He's not calling you anything," I laughed. "He's asking if you speak French."

"Then why doesn't he ask instead of speaking gobbledygook?"

"He is. Listen, do you think a cat speaks like a cow?"

"No," Jim said.

"Then how do you expect a Frenchman to speak like us?"

"A cat isn't a man. A man ought to speak like a man. Not a cow."

I didn't argue any more. Jim had his own way of seeing the world.

CHAPTER FIVE

In the Fog –
A White Lie – Missing Cairo

In three nights we expected to get to Cairo, Illinois. That's where the Ohio River connects with the Mississippi River. We planned to sell the raft in Cairo and board a steamboat up the Ohio into the free states so Jim didn't have to worry anymore about anybody selling him.

The fog rolled in. We knew we couldn't navigate safely, so I jumped into the canoe and pulled the raft through the fog and swift waters towards an island. The island turned out to be nothing more than a high place with a few saplings. Afraid to go on, I tied the raft to a sapling, but the current became too strong, pulled up the sapling, and took Jim and the raft downriver. In only a few seconds, they both disappeared. I called. Jim answered back. In the fog, I couldn't see anything. I tried to catch him. Sometimes he'd be on the left side. I'd paddle towards him. Then he'd be on the right. I'd paddle there. Then I lost him completely. I called, but he didn't answer. Finally, I let the canoe go where it wanted.

When I awoke, the stars twinkled clearly. At first, I thought I had been dreaming, but then I realized what had happened. I worried for Jim. I saw a black speck in the water ahead. I quickly rowed to it, probably a mile downriver, and saw the raft. And sure enough, there was Jim, asleep. I quietly climbed aboard. The hut had almost collapsed. Twigs and sticks littered the raft. It took several pokes before Jim awoke. He began to cry.

"I thought you'd been drowned, child. I didn't know where you'd gone."

"Drowned? Gone? Have you been drinking whiskey?" I asked.

"When would I drink?"

"You're talking so crazy."

"Haven't you been gone?"

"I've been sitting here talking to you—until you fell asleep ten minutes ago."

Jim looked confused. "No," he said. He then told me all about the night according to how he remembered it—how he couldn't find me and how he didn't care if he lived or died after losing me.

"But I never went anywhere, Jim. You must have seen this in a dream."

Jim trusted me more than any person on earth, I think.

"Are you telling me the truth?"

"Yes." I had to fight to keep from laughing.

"Then that's the most frightening dream I've ever had," he said. He then went on to interpret it, telling me what the islands meant, what the fog meant, what the whitewater meant. His face changed. "If I had a dream, then what happened to our hut?"

I couldn't hold it. I laughed until my belly hurt.

Jim looked hurt. "My heart broke because I thought you had drowned," he said. "When you woke me up, I could have kissed your feet. And you want to play me for a fool."

He crawled into what remained of the hut. I tried to get him to come back out, but he wouldn't do it.

After about fifteen minutes, I humbled myself and apologized. I felt so bad I could have kissed his feet.

Jim couldn't wait to get to Cairo because as soon as he got there he'd be a free man. I wanted him to get there, too. Yet, I felt wrong. What had Miss Watson ever done to me, besides trying to teach me to read, that I should treat her this way by helping her slave—her property—escape? But in my mind, Jim didn't seem like property anymore. I felt torn between what I'd been taught and what I felt. I learned two "rights" are not always the same thing. One had to be wrong.

"As soon as I'm free," Jim said, "I'm going to save my money. I'm going to buy my wife from Mr. Blake. Then we'll both work and save. And then we'll buy our two children from Masters Dolan and Crisfield. And if those slave owners don't sell, I'll hire an Abolitionist to steal them."

Such talk put shivers through my spine

because it went against everything I had been taught. I couldn't take it anymore. Surely every white person I knew couldn't be *wrong*. I had to turn Jim in.

"Cairo!" Jim shouted when he saw the lights of a town.

"I'll go ashore," I said.

"You're the best friend I ever had," Jim said. "I've never known a white man to keep his word to me. I'll owe you for my freedom."

Before I could get to shore, two men came by in a skiff.

"Is that your raft up there?" one asked.

"Yes."

"Anybody on it?"

"Yes."

"Black or white?"

I wanted to tell the truth, but I couldn't betray Jim. Something inside me told me *wrong* had to be *right*. "White."

"Five slaves escaped. We've got to capture them before they reach freedom," the other man said. "I think we'll just see for ourselves."

"Please do," I said. "It's my Pap. He's got smallpox. We need help."

"Smallpox!" the first man yelled. "Do you want to infect us?"

"Please, we need help."

"We can't take that chance, boy," the second one said. "Here." The man put a gold piece on a floating slab of wood. "I'll float this twenty dollars to you."

"Add my twenty more," the first man said. "We're afraid to come near even you, son. But we wish you the best."

I cried like I was upset. Then I fished the money from the water. As soon as the men sailed away, I caught up with Jim and showed him the twenty-dollar coins.

I felt good about the money. But I felt awful that I'd lied to those men. And I'd done even *more* wrong—I hadn't turned Jim in. Then I thought how I'd feel if I *had* turned Jim in. I'd feel awful both ways. What's the good of a conscience if you don't feel better after doing one or the other?

Jim saw that I was kinda low. "You be strong, honey. We'll get to Cairo soon enough."

But we didn't get to Cairo. Farther down the river we realized that we were headed down the Mississippi toward Arkansas—farther into slave country. We figured we musta passed the turn up the Ohio River way back in all that fog.

"I should have kept a better watch," I told Jim.

"Don't blame yourself, Huck. You didn't know. We'll figure something out. You just be strong, child. You just be strong."

We made a plan. We would abandon the raft and take the canoe back upriver to Cairo before somebody caught Jim. The sun was rising to the east, so we decided to wait until the next night.

That day we slept. At night, we sneaked to our canoe, but the canoe had disappeared! Because we couldn't make any time pushing the raft upriver against the current, we had no choice but to continue downriver until we could buy a canoe. ("Borrowing" one might send people after us.)

We heard a steamboat. The weather had turned bad, and we lit a lantern so the steamboat wouldn't run us over. Normally, boats traveling upriver stay to the easier shallow water and never get near the swift channel used by vessels going downriver. When fog or bad weather sets in, though, they share the deeper channel, afraid they might run aground in the easier water. That put us both on the same path.

The steamboat came on top of us before we saw her or she saw us.

Bells went off on the steamboat telling the engineer to stop the engines, but before they could stop, the steamboat cut right over our raft. Jim fell overboard on one side and I fell on the other. I dived straight for the bottom to keep from being chopped up by the thirty-foot paddlewheel. I held my breath underwater for

about a minute and a half until my lungs almost burst. When I finally had to shoot up out of the water, the steamboat was tugging up the river, not caring if it had killed us, or what. I called out to Jim, but he never answered. I swam to shore.

I walked about two miles downriver thinking that if Jim had swam to shore, he probably wouldn't trouble himself to swim upstream. Sure enough, there was Jim hiding in a clump of blackberry bushes. I was never so glad to see him! I jumped in the bushes myself. He ran to me and hugged me when he saw me coming. And he had our raft! He said he hadn't heard me calling him because he was too busy swimming downstream trying to catch the raft. We were never both so happy to get back out on the river, in the open—free on the Mississippi.

CHAPTER SIX

A Fallen Duke – A Lost King

For two or three nights, we sailed gently down the river. We relished every minute of it. Nothing matches life on a raft. We watched for candles in passing cabins and used them as our time clock. When they put the last light out in the windows, we knew midnight had come. When the first light appeared again, we knew we had to hide ourselves and the raft.

We found a canoe around the third day. While Jim hid on an island, I took the canoe to the mainland to look for berries to offer a change in our diet. As I paddled up a little creek, two men came running down the bank towards me.

"Save us!" one yelled. "There are dogs after us."

"And men with guns."

"And we didn't do anything!"

They tried to jump into the canoe, but I wouldn't let them. I told them to run up through the brush by the creek, then jump into the water and wade down to the deeper water where I floated. I told them that would throw off the dogs. They did as I told them.

I took them back to the island. Jim helped me fix breakfast.

"So, what got *you* into trouble?" the seventy-year-old man asked the thirty-year-old.

"I sell medicine to take tartar off teeth. Sometimes it takes the enamel off as well. People don't take kindly to it. In the last town I stayed one night longer than I should have. I had to leave in a hurry. That's when I ran into you."

Jim and I looked at each other. The men didn't know one another.

"What about *you*?" asked the younger man.

"I had been preaching a church revival, and making good money at it," the seventy-year-old, bald-headed man said. "I started courting a young lady in the congregation. Unfortunately, her husband found out. A slave woke me up and told me to get out of town quickly."

"Do you think we might work together?" the young one said.

"What do you do?"

"I do several things: Printing, medicine making, theater acting, hypnotizing, fortune telling. I also teach school when somebody lets me. How about you?"

"I'm a doctor by the laying on of hands. I cure cancers and paralysis. I can tell fortunes too if I can hire somebody to check out the facts for me. Mainly, though, I'm a preacher. I save souls."

The young man started crying. Try as we might, we couldn't get him to tell us the problem. Finally, he confessed his true identity.

"I've fallen from grace. It's the secret of my birth. I trust you'll tell no one. By birth, I am a duke. Duke Bridgewater."

I don't know whose eyes got bigger, mine or Jim's. We'd just been reading stories about kings and dukes, and here sat one by our campfire.

"What can we do to get you back to your dukedom?" I asked.

"There is nothing that can be done. Though

it would do me well if you treated me according to my station in life."

"How's that?"

"When you talk to me, call me 'Your Grace' or 'My Lord' or just 'Bridgewater.' Wait on me during meals and do any little thing I want."

We all agreed. By the next day, the old man had turned sour. Finally, *he* started crying.

"I can't go on in this lie," he said. "I must tell who *I* am. The Duke is not the only one thrown from his high place. Can I trust you all?"

We all nodded.

"I am the late disappeared Dauphin, Louis the Seventeen, son of Louis the Sixteen and Mary Antoinette."

"The King of France!" the young man shouted.

Jim and I almost fell over. The King said we could do nothing to help him either, although we could call him 'Your Majesty.' He said when we spoke to him we should bend down on one knee. The King outranked the Duke, so the King expected the Duke to bow as well. We happily waited on them both.

The treatment we gave the King upset the Duke greatly. Finally, the King extended his royal hand.

"We must make peace with each other, my Duke. It's not my fault I'm born a King, nor your fault that you're born a Duke. Let's make the best of this situation in which we find ourselves—plenty of food, an easy life. Let's shake on it."

Before long, I decided we'd found ourselves in the company of two royal liars. I didn't let on to Jim. He fell all over himself waiting on Royalty. If I never learned anything else from Pap, I learned that the best way to get along with his kind of people was to let them have their own way.

CHAPTER SEVEN

Raft Scenes –
A Church Camp Meeting – Acting

The Duke and the King asked us all kinds of questions: Why did we travel only by night? Why did we hide the raft by day? Finally the Duke asked, "Is Jim a runaway slave?"

"Good gracious, no," I said. "Would a runaway slave be running south?"

I told them numerous things about my past, none of which were true. Basically, I "killed everyone off" in my story but me. I said that after everybody died, I had been left with Jim. Because the average boy didn't own a slave, too many people tried to take Jim away from me when we traveled by day. That's why we traveled by night.

The Duke said he would think of a way "to travel by day as people, rather than fugitives."

Ominous clouds formed above us in the night sky. Anticipating a major storm, the King crawled into our raft hut; the Duke followed. Jim had made the hut large enough for only two. Jim and I stood outside as the droplets began to fall. We rode down the river that way the rest of the night. The waves got so strong that at one point I actually fell off the raft. Jim laughed heartily.

The next morning the Duke arose with his carpetbag in hand, from which he produced numerous pieces of paper. One told of "the celebrated Dr. Armand de Montalban of Paris," who could tell people their future.

"That's me," the Duke said, pointing at the picture that looked *nothing* like him.

On another paper he was the "world-famous Shakespearean actor Garrick the Younger, of Drury Lane, London."

On another he proclaimed to be someone else.

And then another.

I almost forgot who he really was.

He pulled out several costumes with frilly sleeves. He told the King that at the next town they would perform scenes from Shakespeare as a duo. "You'll be Juliet."

"How can I be Juliet?" the King asked. "With my bald head and beard?"

"No one will notice. By the way," the Duke said to me, "I've decided how to solve your daylight travel problem. Let's stop at the next town."

When we got to the town, Jim waited with the raft while we went ashore. No one in the town stirred. A slave told us everyone in town was attending a church camp meeting. The King got directions from the slave and said we should join them. The Duke wanted a printing office, which we found. We left him there. I didn't go happily with the King. Everyone always wanted to take me to church, even this scoundrel.

When we got there, we saw almost a thousand people from all over the county. Horses and wagons filled the woods. Lemonade, gingerbread, and watermelon stands were lined up outside. The preaching took place under a huge shed. The preacher held his Bible in the air and told everyone what he held was "the brazen serpent

in the wilderness! Look upon it and live!" He talked the craziest I've ever heard a preacher talk. He screamed. He sweated. He motioned in the air. Pretty soon I couldn't hear him for the noise the people made saying, "Glory!" and "Praise God!" and "Hallelujah!"

The King started praising as well, working his way up towards the front, leaving me behind, and climbing up the stairs. I could hear him yelling over everybody. The preacher told him to speak. The King told everyone he had been a pirate in the Indian Ocean, but after hearing the preacher,

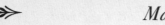

he'd decided to change his ways. He wanted to go back to the Indian Ocean and convert all of those other pirates he knew, but he didn't have any money, but "praise God, somehow God would get him there."

"Take up a collection," someone shouted.

Money started coming forward. Before I knew what had happened, we found ourselves back in the woods running for the raft. The King had collected $87.65 from the crowd. Until he heard the King's figures, the Duke had thought he'd done well in the printing business. He'd sold $9.50 in advertising to people for a newspaper that didn't exist.

While at the office, the Duke had printed a poster. It showed a black man with a bundle over his shoulder. Underneath, he'd printed "$200 reward." The small print told about Jim. Not really about Jim, but a story we all agreed we would follow. We agreed to pretend that Jim had run away from New Orleans and we had captured him to take him back for the reward money. If anyone came along, we would tie Jim in ropes. Jim agreed to the plan.

When it came time for Jim's night watch,

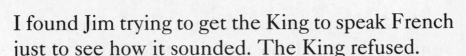

I found Jim trying to get the King to speak French just to see how it sounded. The King refused.

"I've forgotten the language in all this trouble," he said.

Morning came, but, because of the story we'd decided about Jim, we continued to float along. The King practiced his Juliet speech. The Duke made a couple of swords out of strips of wood. He and the King fought with the swords from one end of the raft to the other.

"To make this a truly lively show," the Duke said to the King, "I'll teach you Hamlet's solo speech."

The Duke had to think a moment to remember it—then he began. (I memorized it myself as he taught it to the King because I was so touched by its deepness.)

> *To be, or not to be—that is the bare bodkin*
> *That makes calamity of so long life.*
> *'Tis a consummation devoutly to be wished.*
> *But soft you, the fair Ophelia:*
> *Open not thy ponderous and marble jaws,*
> *But get thee to a nunnery—go!*

At the first town of any size, the Duke had us stop to print small posters that told of the shows. One was for a Shakespeare show, and the other was for something called the Royal Nonesuch (or some such). The Duke and the King entertained Jim and I for the next several days as we floated downriver, looking for a place for our show.

"This is a large enough town," the Duke finally said, somewhere in Arkansas. "Forget Shakespeare. Let's give them something they'll *really* remember."

All over Bricksville, the King and Duke put up notices of the show that read:

AT THE COURT HOUSE!

THREE NIGHTS ONLY!

The World-Famous Tragic Actors
DAVID GARRICK THE YOUNGER!

EDMUND KEAN THE ELDER!
*Of the London
and Continental Theatres,*
In their Thrilling Tragedy of
THE KING'S CAMELEOPARD,
or
THE ROYAL NONESUCH! ! !
Admission 50 cents.

LADIES AND CHILDREN
NOT ADMITTED

"There," said the Duke. "If that last line doesn't bring them in, I don't know Arkansas."

⚔—⚔—

That night, the Duke took tickets from a crowd of men like I'd never seen. He praised the show, lifted the curtain, and said, "I now present to you, here for three nights only, direct from London, the greatest tragedy ever told: The King's Cameleopard."

The King pranced onstage on all fours—all but naked! He'd been painted all over in rings and stripes the same colors as a rainbow.

The audience howled. It was the funniest thing I'd ever seen. The King finished and hurried offstage. The crowd called him back. He did the show again. They laughed even harder. He hurried offstage. The crowd called him back. They couldn't get enough. The Duke lowered the curtain. "Thank you for coming."

"That's it?" one man shouted.

"That's all."

"Royal Nonesuch, I'll say!" yelled one man.

"We've been tricked!" twenty people shouted. They stormed the stage.

One man yelled, "Gentlemen! Stop! We've been made fools of, our money's taken, but no

one needs to know it. Let's tell everyone what a great show this is. That way, they'll be fools as much as we."

All agreed to the idea.

After the men left, the Duke suggested to the King that it might be a good idea not to do any more shows. For one night's work we made $465.

When we left Jim, we tied him in ropes. Sometimes we'd leave him for hours. He grew tired of it. The Duke said he'd come up with a different solution.

The next morning the Duke outfitted Jim in a King Lear costume, a white wig and whiskers, and painted Jim's head and hands with blue makeup that made Jim look like he'd been dead for a couple of weeks. He nailed a sign to the raft that said:

Sick Arab – but harmless when not out of his head

The Duke told Jim—if approached—to come out of the hut acting crazy and no one would likely bother him.

With the money we had made, the King bought us fancy clothes. He explained, "There may come a time when we need them."

CHAPTER EIGHT

Getting Information –
The Grand Performance

One morning the King told me to get my
fancy clothes on. He and the Duke had dressed
in theirs. The King hadn't thought of a plan yet
for making more money, but said one would
come to him. He needed to check out the lay of
the town. To present an image, we needed to
arrive in style, so the King had me guide upriver
three miles towards a loading steamboat.

Along the way we spotted a young man with
traveling bags. The King invited him aboard our
canoe, since he was headed for the same
steamboat as us. The man at first mistook the

King for someone named Mr. Harvey Wilks, which the King took note of. The King began questioning him about this "Mr. Wilks."

"Mr. Wilks is in passage from England," the young man said, "to see his ill brother, Peter. But I'm sad to say that Mr. Wilks waited too long. Peter died. He left money in a Will to Mr. Wilks. Mr. Wilks will certainly find himself blessed when he arrives. Not to mention the three girls."

"Three girls?" asked the King.

"Yes. They belonged to another brother of Peter and Mr. Wilks. That brother died a year ago and Peter had been taking care of them. Mary Jane's sixteen, Susan's fifteen, and Joanna's fourteen. She's the one who looks odd, but she gives herself to good works. Being a preacher, Mr. Wilks will recognize her good character."

I saw the twinkle in the King's eyes.

"There is another brother, as well," the man said, "who should be coming with Mr. Wilks. His name is William. He is a deaf-mute—and so, of course, cannot hear or speak."

The King went on to questioning the man, all about Peter Wilks's good friends and neighbors, till he about emptied him.

After we dropped off the young man at the steamboat, our "names" changed. The King became Mr. Harvey Wilks. The Duke became the deaf-mute brother, William. I became the servant. Jim minded the raft and carried on like a madman.

We boarded the steamboat and sailed downriver four miles to the town. Some men greeted us. The King told them we had arrived from England. The men offered the bad news of Peter's death. The King cried and wailed. He made all sorts of hand signals in the air, pretending to talk sign language. Suddenly the Duke began crying, but in a silent way. It was the darndest performance I'd ever seen. It made me ashamed of the entire human race.

When we got to the house, the three girls waited on the porch. As they saw who they *thought* were their uncles, they ran to them. Everybody cried. The King and the Duke played it in perfect sorrow, kneeling before the coffin and praying. The Duke, being mute, shed only

tears while the King added words. I've never seen anything so disgusting.

After the King gave a little speech about our journey, the crowd that had gathered began singing. Then the King met with several people in the crowd, going on and on about names and stories he read in letters from his brother who was now dead. (He was just saying the same words we had heard from the young man that we picked up on the river. He had a very good memory.)

Since the brothers had arrived from England, the Will could be read. The dead man gave the house and $3,000 to the girls, and a business, other rental houses, and $3,000 to the two living brothers (the King and the Duke). It also told where the $6,000 in cash had been hidden downstairs in the basement. The King insisted that he, the Duke, and I go down and get it. Instead of bringing it up, the King wanted to count it.

"We want to be up and up and make sure it's all here," he said.

The count revealed we were $415 short.

"We can't go upstairs without the whole $6,000," the King said. "They'll think we stole it.

Empty your pockets and make up the difference. I don't want anyone upstairs to suspect us."

The Duke emptied his pockets, as did the King. They both grumbled about why the dead fool would say there was $6,000 here when there'd only been $5,585. It took most of the money they'd made from the Cameleopard show to bring the balance to $6,000.

"Now we'll take it upstairs," the Duke said, "and count it in front of everybody and give it to the girls in a big show. The crowd will go crazy."

I followed them up.

"Friends," the King said, "our dead brother was a giving man, but we don't need this money. We give it all to these three young ladies, the apples of their Uncle Peter's eyes."

The crowd cheered and cried.

"Hogwash," a booming voice shouted from the back of the crowd.

"Doctor Robinson!" someone called out.

"Ah! You are the good Doctor," the King said to him with his hand out. "My dear brother wrote of you."

"Get your hand away from me. You're telling nothing but lies. You're a fraud! You don't know

Peter Wilks any more than a monkey knows the alphabet. Girls, these men are frauds. I advise you to order them out of your house at once."

Mary Jane, the eldest girl, stepped forward. "Doctor, I cannot believe your tone at our Uncle Peter's death. Our uncles have traveled so far, all the way from England, to be with us. They've done everything to unselfishly prove themselves. They've even given us their inheritance, leaving them with nothing. I know these are my uncles." She smiled at the King and the Duke. They smiled back. It made me sick to see it. "I'm giving them the entire $6,000." She handed over the cash. "Invest this for us. We trust you completely."

"Pig's eyes!" The doctor stormed from the house.

CHAPTER NINE

Hiding in the Room –
Hiding the Money

After the crowd left, Mary Jane gave Uncle William (the Duke) the spare room and gave her own room to Uncle Harvey (the King).

"I'll sleep on a cot in my sisters' room," Mary Jane said.

They put me in the attic.

The girls prepared a large supper. I waited on the Duke and King. The household slaves waited on everyone else. Afterwards, I ate leftovers in the kitchen with the youngest girl, Joanna. She quizzed me about England. I must say I did poorly under the exam.

"I don't believe *anything* you've told me," Joanna said. "You're a liar." She said this as Mary Jane and Susan came into the kitchen.

"Joanna!"

Joanna turned sheepishly towards Mary Jane's voice.

"This young man is our guest," Mary Jane said. "A servant to our uncles. You apologize to him immediately."

"But he said..."

"I don't care what he said. Apologize."

Joanna protested. Mary Jane railed into her. Susan followed. Finally, beaten down, Joanna apologized. What a long-winded and sincere apology it was. I wanted to lie again just to hear it one more time.

I couldn't help but feel badly. Mary Jane and Susan trusted me. Joanna had humbled herself before me. I couldn't let the King and the Duke rob them. I told everyone I wanted to go to bed.

I left them downstairs and then climbed to the attic to think about what I should do. If I confided in Doctor Robinson, he might turn me in along with the two scoundrels. If I told the girls, they might do the same. I decided the only way out of this was to steal the money myself, hide it, leave town with the Duke and King, and then write the girls a note when we had traveled beyond harm's way, telling them where to find the money. I hurried down to the King's room.

I heard the King and the Duke coming up the stairs. I started to hide under the bed, but then decided instead to hide among Mary Jane's dresses. I made a good choice because as soon as they came into the room, the Duke checked under the bed.

"I'm worried about that doctor," the Duke said. "I think we should leave tonight with the money. Let's not be greedy."

"Before we sell off the property?" the King asked. "That's an extra eight or nine thousand dollars."

"We've got more than enough. Why take everything belonging to these poor orphans? Let's leave while it's safe."

"Don't worry for the orphans," the King said. "Once we sell off the property and leave with the money, the buyers of the properties will feel sorry for the girls and return everything to them.

The only ones out will be the buyers. It's the cost of being a fool. Besides, these girls are young—they've got the rest of their lives to work."

I couldn't stand listening to them talk this way.

"I guess you're right," the Duke said. "But I don't like where we've hidden the money."

My ears perked.

"If someone cleans the room, they may find it and keep a bit."

"You're right," the King said. He crossed to where I stood. I thought of what I'd say if he found me. He removed a large box about three feet from my leg. Opening the box, he removed the sack of money. "Let's hide it under the bed. The only way someone would find it there is if they flipped the mattress."

They left. I lifted the mattress and took the sack of money. I carried it upstairs to the attic. I knew better than to hide the money in the house. If it came up missing, the Duke and the King would tear the place apart. I waited for everyone to go to bed. When the house got quiet, I took the money and slipped downstairs.

Everyone slept soundly, including the men downstairs sitting with the corpse. I crossed to the front door. Someone had locked it and I didn't have a key. I heard someone coming down the stairs, so I hurried into the parlor where the corpse lay in a coffin. There was no place to hide the money. Finally, I stuffed the sack under the lid of the coffin. Then I hid behind the door.

Mary Jane came into the room. She prayed over the coffin. When she'd gone and all became quiet, I hurried to the attic.

What an ideal plan! The money would be buried along with the body. After we were down the river, I'd write to Mary Jane. They would dig up the body and get their money back. But then I worried that the man who nailed the lid on the coffin might see the money first. He'd give it back to the King. The King would never let the money out of his sight again. I couldn't go back downstairs. If the men woke up and caught me with the money, the King would let me hang. I didn't sleep at all that night.

The next day everyone gathered for the funeral. Another thought crossed my mind:

What if somebody stole the money off the dead man last night and it wasn't there anymore? When I write to Mary Jane and she digs up the body, maybe all she'll find is a dead man. I didn't dare look to see if the dead man still had the money stuffed between his legs, but it sure was on my mind.

The preacher spoke. Someone played a rented organ. The crowd of mourners sang. The King gave a long speech. Everyone cried. I never heard so much nose-blowing in all my life. When it came time to seal the coffin, I held my breath. The lid went on. The nails went in. They buried the body.

After hugging everybody, the King said he had an announcement. "I'm taking the girls with me back to England. What better place to be than with one's family?"

Everyone, including the girls, was thrilled at the idea.

"We must, of course, sell all the property, including the houses and the slaves," he added.

The next day slave traders bought two boy slaves and shipped them to Memphis. The traders sent the boys' mother to New Orleans. I thought about Jim and how he missed his family. It was terrible to break up a family this way. Some of the townspeople thought it cruel as well, including the Duke. He told the King so afterwards.

"They'll be back," the King said, "when everyone realizes what we've done." I didn't believe the King. It seemed to me that the mother and her children had been broken up for good.

The next day the house was to be sold at auction. I awoke that morning to the King shaking me.

"Have you been in my room?" he asked.

"No."

"Have you seen anyone in my room?"

"Just the slaves."

"The ones we sold?"

"Yes."

The King's face turned so red he looked like a pickled beet.

"Confound it."

"What?" I asked, playing innocent.

"You never mind."

The Duke started arguing with the King. The King fussed at the Duke. I thought they were going to fight right there. They disappeared down the stairs and left me alone in the attic.

CHAPTER TEN

Revealing the Fraud–Another Plan

As I passed the sisters' bedroom the next morning, I heard Mary Jane crying. She told me she felt sorry for the slave family that had been separated. "Mother and two children will never see each other again," she sobbed.

I couldn't take it. "They will," I said before I could catch myself. "They'll be back together in two weeks. If we act quickly."

She hugged me. "How do you know?"

I couldn't think of anything fast enough so I tried something I'd never done before: I told the truth. "It takes several days for money to change hands to make sales final. Mary Jane, is there anywhere you could go for the afternoon?"

"Yes. Mr. Lothrop's. Why?"

"If I tell you how the slaves will come back together, and prove to you how I know, will you go to Lothrop's?"

She nodded.

"Do you mind if I shut the door?"

She agreed.

"When I tell you this, you've got to be quiet."

She nodded.

"Those uncles of yours are frauds."

She waited to hear me out. I told her everything (except for *one* part that concerned a certain coffin…).

She jumped from the bed and cried, "We'll have those men tarred and feathered, right this minute."

"Please don't," I begged. "If you did, I'd be fine. But there's *another* person that would be hurt terribly if you didn't wait." I thought about Jim when I said this. If the Duke and the King knew I had betrayed them, they'd sell Jim back into slavery in a minute. "How far is it to Mr. Lothrop's?"

"Four miles."

"Go visit him and come back tonight. If you get here before eleven o'clock, put a candle in the window. If I'm not back here by eleven, it means I'm safe and gone. When you know I'm gone, tell the neighbors and have these two jailed. If something happens and I don't get away, though, I hope you'll stand by me."

"Of course I will."

"If I get away, I won't be here to prove these men aren't your uncles." I took some paper off Susan's desk and wrote:

Royal Nonesuch, Cameleopard, Bricksville

I handed her the paper. "You contact the town of Bricksville, show them this paper, and you'll have an entire town down here to tell you who these actors are. Let the auction go on today as planned. No money will change hands for a couple of days so nobody will be hurt."

"I'll do just as you say," she said. "I'll go down to breakfast and then straight to Mr. Lothrop's."

"No. You can't go to breakfast. You have to go now. Those trained crooks will look right in your face and know I told you. They'll slide away quicker than a snake. You leave now. I'll make up

something about why you're gone. I'll tell your sisters. There's one more thing. The money."

"I know," she said. "They've got it. We'll just have to get it back."

"*They* don't have it."

"Who *does*?"

I couldn't tell her because I knew she'd never make it out of the house without squealing. I got another piece of paper and wrote down the truth. It took me awhile because I write slowly and I wrote the entire story of how I hid the money between her dead uncle's legs. I folded up the paper and gave it to her.

"I'm giving you this to read on your way to Lothrop's. Please don't think poorly of me. I did the best I could considering the circumstances."

"Good-bye," she said. "I'll do everything just as you've told me. I'll think of you often. And I'll pray for you."

Pray for me? I thought, *If she knew me she'd probably want to pray for something a little easier*, but I kept quiet.

I found the sisters sitting around the breakfast table. The uncles were still upstairs, but I had to talk quickly.

"Mary Jane had to leave," I said. "Someone has taken ill at—at the neighbor's house."

"I hope it's not Hannah!"

"Yes, it is," I said. "They stayed up with her all night last night. She may not make it. She has the mumps."

"People don't die from the mumps," Joanna said.

"It's got other things mixed in," I said. "Measles, whooping cough, consumption, yellow jaundice, brain fever. It's a bad mix. Highly catching. Few have ever seen it, not even the doctor. Mary Jane said not to tell your uncles. If your uncles knew she'd visited Hannah on her catchy deathbed, they might postpone the trip to England."

"They *can't* know," Susan agreed. "We can't miss England just to wait around to see if Mary Jane comes down with... whatever it is. And I've already packed my bags."

"Exactly," I answered. "Mary Jane said for you to tell the uncles that she'd gone to tell some people to come to the auction."

The sisters did as I instructed them. The uncles didn't seem to care where Mary Jane was.

Later that day, everything sold at the auction. The uncles smiled until a crowd of folks came up yelling and laughing. Someone called out:

"Here are the *other* brothers of old Peter Wilks! Which set do you think is *real*?"

The Real Uncles –
Digging Up the Truth

The crowd brought a nice-looking older gentleman and a nice-looking younger gentleman over to see the King and the Duke. The younger man had his right arm in a sling.

I felt myself wilting, but the smiling King reached out his hand, as he would greet anybody. The older gentleman didn't take it.

"My name is Harvey Wilks," the older gentleman said. "I'm the brother of Peter Wilks, deceased. This is our other brother, William. He can't hear or speak, and with his hand broken it is impossible for him to communicate. Our baggage unfortunately left the boat in the town before this one, but when it comes we will prove we are truly the proper relatives."

He sounded English to me by the way he pronounced words.

"When did *you* come to town?" a man asked the King. I'd never seen this man before.

"About an hour before sundown the day before the funeral."

"How'd you come?"

"On the *Susan Powell*," the King said. "From Cincinnati."

"Then how come I saw you up at the Point that same morning? You were in a canoe. And you had a boy with you."

They started arguing.

"Would you know the boy again if you saw him?" Doctor Robinson asked.

"Probably not. Why, yes! There he is." He pointed at me.

"Neighbors," the doctor said, "I've told you before these men are frauds. Let's go down to the hotel with both sets of uncles and have this out."

It was almost sundown when the doctor began. He pointed at the King and the Duke.

"If these two men are *frauds*, they may have help waiting to get the money out of town. If these men are for *real*, I'm sure they won't mind if we guard their money for them. Would you?"

"Gentlemen," the King began, "the slaves we sold have *stolen* our money out of our bedroom. You won't find it at the house." The King looked sincere because he thought himself to be telling the truth.

By the crowd's reaction, I could tell we lost support.

The doctor turned to me and asked, "Are you English as well?"

"Yes."

They started asking me all sorts of quizzes about England, which I tried to answer.

"That's enough," the doctor said. "You're not a very good liar, young man."

I was happy he stopped asking me questions, but I didn't take kindly to his compliment.

"I know how to solve this," Harvey Wilks proclaimed. "My brother had a tattoo on his chest. Surely the undertaker can confirm this."

"Wait," said the lawyer, Mr. Levi Bell. He pointed at the King. "What was the tattoo?"

"A blue arrow."

"Wrong!" shouted Harvey Wilks. "It was his initials, PBW."

"There was no tattoo at all," the grave undertaker said.

The crowd gasped.

"Enough!" Levi shouted over the yelling crowd. "We'll dig up the corpse and see."

They dragged us to the graveyard. Thunder and lightning began. Rain fell in buckets. I wished I had Jim close by to tell me if these things were a good sign, or bad. I had my own idea.

Finally, they brought the coffin up and opened the lid.

"The money!" a man shouted. He held up a bag.

The man holding me loosened his grip to get a better look. I made a beeline through the crowd and down the vacant street. As I ran by the Wilks's house, I saw a candle in the window. I wanted to stop, but I ran on. I would have liked to have said good-bye to Mary Jane.

When I reached the river, I borrowed a canoe someone had forgotten to tie down and rowed madly to the raft.

"Jim!" I shouted as I climbed aboard.

Suddenly, something dead-for-weeks came out of the hut, calling, "Huck! Huck!"

I screamed and fell back into the water before I remembered Jim's makeup. Jim wanted to hug me.

"Save it for breakfast," I said, scrambling. "Let's get out of here!"

When the lightning struck again, I received a horror of a different kind—*the Duke and the King had followed us on a raft of their own!*

CHAPTER TWELVE

Royal Pains –
Jim Is Stolen – Huck's Decision

The King grabbed me. "Tired of being with us? Tell me what you had in mind."

I had to think quickly before the King shook my head off. "The man holding me felt sorry for me. When everyone shifted to look at the money, he told me to run. He said I couldn't help either of you. I hated leaving you behind. Jim did, too."

"That's right," Jim said.

"I didn't address you," the King said. "I should drown you in the river."

"Let go of that boy," the Duke said. "Did *you* ask about him—or me—when *you* hightailed for the river?"

The King let me loose. "That blamed town."

"You should better blame *yourself*," the Duke said, glaring at the King. "A clever trick—hiding the money in a casket!"

"Me?" the King asked angrily. "What about *you?*"

"I have to give you that," the Duke said. "But when you ditched the boy and me, you were going to sneak back to the town, dig up the body, and keep the stash yourself. I should drown *you* in the river!"

"*You're* the scoundrel with the plan!"

The King lunged at the Duke. They fought all over the raft. One choked one, the other choked the other. Jim and I did our own dance to keep from getting knocked into the water.

"Admit it!" the Duke yelled.

"I admit it," the King said as the Duke squeezed the King's neck so hard the King's head turned blue.

Later, they huddled in the hut, each forgiven, sleeping soundly.

I told Jim the whole story.

The Duke and the King tried several frauds in different villages along the way. They started a dancing school, but when the townsfolk saw they danced like kangaroos, they waltzed them out of town. They tried so many schemes, I can't remember them all: playing as missionaries, hypnotizing, lecturing, teaching, doctoring, fortune telling. They spent every cent they had. We hated being with them.

They began talking quietly just to each other, making Jim and me nervous. Then, when we came upon a little town named Pikesville, the King told us to stay put while he went to shore. At noon we were to find him.

Noon came and the Duke and I found the King in a saloon. A bunch of men were arguing with the King, and the Duke jumped into the fight. I took the chance and *ran*.

When I'd rowed the canoe back to the raft, I yelled, "Let's go, Jim! Let's get out of here! We're rid of them. Jim! Jim?"

I couldn't find Jim!

Halfway back to town, I asked a boy if he'd seen a black man matching Jim's description.

"You mean the dangerous runaway slave? He's

chained down at Silas Phelps's," the boy said. "A man…" (he went on to describe the King) "…found him first, but sold him for $40 to ol' man Burton rather than waiting to collect the full $200 reward. Then Burton sold him to Phelps. I saw the slave's picture on a New Orleans wanted poster."

I thought of the poster the Duke had printed.

I stumbled back to the raft. Jim would be a much better slave at *home* than down South.

But if I wrote to Miss Watson and told her where Jim was... why, for the rest of my life I'd be known as a blasted Abolitionist. I'd be known as somebody who helped a black slave try to get his freedom. And for the rest of Jim's life, he'd be treated as a slave who'd tried to escape, living a life lower than a stray dog's. The law said Jim was a slave. All the respectable people I knew would say I was doing wrong by helping him escape. So, I *had* to turn Jim back to Miss Watson, his rightful owner. If I didn't, I would be sinning and I could end up burning in the "Bad Place." That scared me. I took out a piece of paper and wrote:

Miss Watson, your runaway slave Jim is down here two miles below Pikesville, and Mr. Phelps has got him and he will give him up for the reward if you send.

HUCK FINN

I felt good. I felt washed of my sins. I prayed and believed God heard. And then I thought of Jim. I thought of days and nights together. I thought of conversations, songs, laughs. I thought how he'd let *me* sleep, instead of getting sleep himself. I remembered how glad he was to see me, if I'd been gone five minutes or five days. I remembered how he called me "honey" and "child." I remembered he said I was his best friend ever...

"I'd rather burn in the Bad Place!"

I grabbed that paper and tore it up.

"Jim will be a free man, whatever cost I have to pay to see it done."

I put on my suit the King had bought me. I rowed the canoe to shore, filled it with rocks, and sunk it, so no one would find it until I came back.

I saw the Duke as I sneaked back through town. While I watched, he tacked a poster on a tree for another "Cameleopard" show. *The Royal Nonesuch was at it again*, I thought.

Whatever the future held for me, I had only one place to find: Silas Phelps's where Jim was held. No matter what it took—risking my own life even—Jim would be a free man.

CHAPTER THIRTEEN

My New "Aunt Sally"– Tom Foolery

When I got to Silas Phelps's farm, it looked like Sunday. Everything was quiet, except for the breeze and bugs.

"Might as well get on with this," I mumbled.

I climbed over the fence and started towards the back of the kitchen. When I got about halfway, a hound growled behind me. More hounds came from the corners. Before I knew it, there were fifteen around me in a circle.

"You dogs get," a black woman said as she came from the kitchen. She swung a rolling pin in her hand. Those dogs lost themselves in a minute.

Three little black children ran behind the woman and, when she stopped, they grabbed her dress and looked around. A white woman appeared at the door. She had three little white children and they acted just like the black ones. The white woman burst into tears and ran towards me.

"It's you!"

"Yes'm," I said as she hugged me.

"Children, it's your cousin Tom! We've been expecting you for a couple of days. Did your boat run aground?"

"Yes'm."

"Don't say 'yes'm.' " She ruffled my hair. "Say 'Aunt Sally.' "

OK, I now have an Aunt Sally, I thought.

"You must have seen your uncle on the way here," she said. "He's gone to town to fetch you. We've gone every day for the past week."

"I got here early so I took my time coming the back way. That's how I must have missed him."

"But where's your luggage?"

"I hid it."

"It'll be stolen."

"Not where I hid it." What I really wanted to do was to get my "cousins" outside and pump

them for information.

"I've been running on and on," Aunt Sally said. "I'll stop talking. Tell me about Sis and the family."

I knew I was up a tree and hanging on the last limb. Just when I thought I'd have to try truth for the second time in my life, I heard a horse *clop-clop-clop* down the road. The woman grabbed me and hid me behind the bed.

"Here comes Silas. We'll play a joke on him. Children, don't you say a word."

I prayed Silas didn't find Tom down at the dock, otherwise there'd be two of us.

"Did you find him?" Aunt Sally asked Silas when he walked in.

"No. I'm beginning to worry."

"What could have happened to him?"

"That's just it."

"Why, Silas! Look yonder."

He looked out the window. Sally hurriedly pulled me up. He turned around.

"Who's *that*?"

"Who do you think it is?" she asked.

I prayed he recognized me as well as Aunt Sally had.

"I don't know," he said. "Who is it?"

"It's Tom Sawyer."

I almost passed out from joy. They thought I was my old buddy Tom. I gladly told them all about everyone back home and the riverboat ride down. They never suspected me, but my confidence shook when I heard the steamboat whistle. What if Tom were aboard that boat?

"I better get my luggage," I told them.

"Silas will go with you."

"No," I said. "I wouldn't trouble you, if I could drive the wagon myself."

I started up the road. In about a mile, I saw a wagon. Sure enough, Tom Sawyer rode as passenger. I'd never seen him so dressed up. I hailed it down.

Tom's mouth dropped. His eyes grew wide. "I've never done you any harm, Huck Finn. Why are you back, you ghost?"

"I'm not back. I never left."

When he heard my voice he eased up. "You're not dead?"

"No. Feel me."

He got out of the wagon, reached up, and touched me. "Huck!"

He had his driver wait while we drove in my wagon up the road a little and talked. I told him my situation, except for the part about Jim.

"You be me," Tom insisted. "Take my trunk for your luggage. I'll show up later."

"What will you say?"

"Leave that to me," Tom said. I did. With Tom and tricks, a body didn't have to have any worries.

"There's one more thing, Tom. I'm stealing a slave. Miss Watson's Jim…"

"What!"

"I know it's wrong," I said. "I've got to anyway. I'm going to set him free."

Tom grinned. "I'll help you steal him!"

About half an hour after I got back, Tom's wagon stopped in front of the house.

"Silas, there's a stranger outside."

The wagon disappeared back down the road. Tom climbed the fence and walked to the front porch like he owned the place.

"Mr. Archibald Nichols, I presume," Tom said with a tip of his hat.

"I'm sorry, son," Silas said. "Your driver dropped you three miles short. Come in, have supper with us, and I'll take you on."

While we ate, Tom talked about how his name was William Thompson from Hicksville, Ohio. I never heard such hogwash. He could run on more than a mountain spring.

Then, right in the middle of a sentence, Tom got up and kissed Aunt Sally on the mouth! Sally jumped up from her chair, wiping and spitting.

"How dare you!"

"I'm sorry, ma'am," Tom said. "They told me you'd like it."

"What do you take me for?" She picked up a spinning stick. I thought any minute she'd crack him over the head.

"Everybody said…"

"Who's everybody?" Sally asked. "You had better say their names or this world's going to be one idiot short."

Tom turned to Silas. "Didn't you think she'd like it?"

"No. I believe not."

"Tom," (Tom looked at me.) "didn't *you* think Aunt Sally would open her arms and say, 'Sid Sawyer'?"

"My land," Sally screamed as she grabbed him. "You rascal."

Tom Sawyer played like he was his own brother while I played like I was Tom.

"I didn't know you were coming, too, Sid," I said to Tom.

We didn't ask about Jim the whole meal, but somehow the topic worked itself around. One of Sally's boys asked, "Can Tom and Sid go with us to see the show?"

"No one's going to the show," Silas said. "That runaway slave told Burton that the people producing it were scandalous. The town's going to tar and feather them if what the slave says is true."

Tom and I were supposed to share a bedroom. We asked to go to bed early. We went upstairs, slid down the lightning rod, and hurried to town. Until we could find where Silas had hidden Jim, I wanted to warn the King and the Duke—so when *their* plans got messed up they wouldn't mess up *mine*.

I saw the townspeople pulling the King and the Duke up Main Street. A man told me the audience had waited for the King to get his clothes off before the town jumped them. Both scoundrels had been tarred, feathered, tied to logs, and dragged about town. They looked like two overgrown chickens on a stick.

Human beings can be awful cruel to one another.

CHAPTER FOURTEEN

Jim Is Found –
Tom's Escape Plot

On the way home, Tom stopped me on the road. "I've figured out where Jim is."

"Where?" I asked. We'd seen no sign of him.

"Do you remember when that slave took that dog slop down to the hut with the lean-to? By the ash hopper? Did you notice that piece of fruit?"

"Dogs don't eat fruit," I said.

"And the slave unlocked the door? Afterwards, he gave Uncle Silas the key."

"I saw that."

"Fruit? A locked door? That means somebody's kept prisoner in there."

"It's got to be Jim," I said.

"This is how we're going to get him out," Tom said. I would explain Tom's plan in detail, but like most of Tom's plans, it would change itself completely before it got to the end.

"And don't bring up more reasons why I shouldn't help you set Jim free," Tom ordered firmly. "You've gone on and on about my family, about people back home, about what they'd think of me if I go through with this. I know people would say it's not respectable, but I gave you my word, didn't I? Beyond that, I've got my own reasons. Don't you think I've thought about all those things? If I keep my word, that's respectable enough for you, isn't it?"

I still didn't understand why he'd agreed to help me. He had to know what we were about to do was wrong.

The next morning, Tom and I went down to the slave cabins to pet the dogs and make friends with Nat, the slave that fed Jim—if it *was* Jim that was being fed. As the slave loaded up a plate with food, we asked him why he tied his hair up with little ringlets of string.

"To keep the witches away," Nat said.

"Do you have a problem with witches?" Tom asked.

"They're everywhere," the man said. "Last night I heard them whispering outside."

I looked at Tom. The "them" was us whispering! Good thing this man hadn't caught us! We were out searching in the dark for Jim.

"But the dogs didn't bark," Nat added.

No wonder, I thought. *We were petting them.*

"Ya feeding your dog?" Tom asked.

"Of sorts," the slave said. "You want to see him?"

As we walked towards the ash hopper with Nat, I whispered to Tom, "This isn't part of the original plan."

"Plans change."

I didn't like it.

As soon as the door opened, Jim bellowed out, "Huck! And Lord, if it isn't Tom Sawyer."

"Does he know you?" Nat asked.

"What would make you think that?" Tom asked quickly.

"He called you by name."

"I didn't hear him."

"I didn't hear him," I repeated.

"Did you call our names?" Tom asked Jim.

"No," Jim said, playing along.

"It's those witches!" the slave screamed.

"You've got it awful bad," Tom said. Tom gave the poor man a dime. "You need to buy more string and tie your hair tighter."

While Tom talked with Nat, I whispered to Jim, "Don't ever let on you know us. We're going to set you free."

That night, we slid down the lightning rod. We sneaked into the lean-to next to the hut and started digging with our knives. Tom said where we dug was right behind Jim's bed. When we finally dug all the way through, no one would notice because Jim's sheets would hide the evidence. We scratched away until midnight, our hands blistered up, and we were no further along than if we'd kicked the ground with our feet.

"This isn't going to work, Huck. Hand me your knife."

He already had his knife, but I handed him mine anyway.

He threw it down!

"Hand me your *knife*. I want to be able to *say* I dug Jim out with a... *knife*."

I thought he'd lost his mind. Then I understood. I handed him a pick-axe.

I grabbed the shovel. We made good time then.

The next night, within two hours of digging, we emerged beneath Jim's bed. We crawled out, lit a candle, and awoke Jim. He called us "honey" and "child" and hugged us. He wanted us to get something to cut his ankle chain. I could see it was only looped around a leg of the bed.

"No," Tom said. "We can't rush things. Jim, be on the lookout. We'll be sending you things to help you escape on your own."

I began to wonder if I had made the right decision allowing Tom Sawyer to help me. I wanted Jim to escape. Tom wanted to make a game of it.

The next morning, Tom pushed a candle through a piece of cornbread that was going to Jim. When Nat took Jim the cornbread, we went along to see how Tom's smuggling idea would work. Jim bit down on the cornbread and nearly broke out all his teeth. (Never again did Jim eat anything without first stabbing it a few times.)

Before Jim could finish his meal, hounds started pouring out from under Jim's bed. There must have been fifteen of them. They'd smelled Jim's cornbread and come from the hole we'd dug. We'd forgotten to close the door to the lean-to on the other side.

Nat yelled "Witches!" once, keeled over on the floor, and started screaming. Tom opened the door and threw the cornbread out. The dogs followed. I ran around to the lean-to and shut the door. When we both came back, Nat was still kicking on the ground.

"What happened, Nat?" Tom asked.

"I saw witches again. They looked like the Devil's Dogs."

"You need a witch pie."

"I don't know how to make a witch pie."

"You don't?" Tom asked. "I'll make one for you."

CHAPTER FIFTEEN

Pie and Rats –
Grand Escape – Jim's Decision

Tom said he had the escape worked out, but Jim and I would have to give him time. He said if we freed Jim now, he might not get far without the whole escape route plotted out. Unfortunately, Tom was right.

Tom found a couple of nails he said a prisoner could use to write on a dungeon wall.

"Jim can't write."

"Doesn't matter," Tom said.

Tom stole some spoons and a sheet as well. He tore up the sheet and made a rope ladder with the strips. Finally, we took some flour from the house and baked the rope ladder in a pan we'd taken out of the attic. We had too much ladder for one pan. In fact, we had enough ladder for a whole meal. Tom threw the extra ladder away, took the pie to Nat, and said, "This is the witch pie. Give it to the runaway slave."

When Jim found the rope ladder in the pie, I could tell he'd thought we'd lost our minds.

Tom still hadn't told me his plan.

Tom insisted we make pens out of nails so Jim could write his name in blood. He said he had read it in books.

"You need a coat of arms," Tom said.

"I don't have a coat of any kind," Jim answered.

"You'll have one before this day is out."

While Jim and I worked making pens, Tom wrote on a piece of paper.

"I've designed your coat of arms," he said. "We'll have a bend, that's a fess, with a dog, that's a couchant, with his foot on a chain, and a motto, *Maggiore fretta, minore atto*. I got it out of a book— it means *the more haste the less speed.*"

Tom might as well have spoken French. He tried to explain some things to us, but refused to explain others.

"Jim needs to write sad love poems on the wall," Tom said.

"Love poems? Jim can't write," I said.

"You can scratch them out for him. Jim can carve out what you write and then add the blood."

~ ~ ~

The next morning, we caught fifteen of the wildest rats one could ever hope for. We hid them in a cage under Aunt Sally's bed. While we looked for spiders, one of the children opened the door of the cage to see if the rats would come out. They did. We found Aunt Sally standing on the bed, screaming. The rats did their best to entertain her. We caught about a dozen more, but these weren't as lively as the first batch.

We captured spiders, bugs, frogs, and caterpillars. We tried to get a hornet's nest, but the hornets were still home. We caught a dozen garter snakes and put them in our room. I guess we didn't tie the bag tight enough, because after dinner, the bag was empty. For the next

week, snakes dropped from the ceiling and showed up in bed. At night, we could hear Aunt Sally screaming all the way to Jericho like the house was afire.

Jim did a good imitation of Aunt Sally when Tom dumped everything into Jim's hut. Jim tore the chain loose and climbed out through the hole into the lean-to. It took forever for Tom to persuade Jim to go back into the hut.

"One more day," Tom said. "A servant girl has to deliver unsigned letters to warn the family of trouble."

"What servant girl? Why do we want to warn the family? That doesn't make sense."

"That's the way the books say it's done. If you don't do this, Huck, I won't tell you the rest of the plan. Jim won't get away. Are you in?"

What choice did I have?

Tom dressed me in one of Aunt Sally's dresses and the "servant girl" wedged a message on the back door:

Beware. Trouble is brewing. Keep a sharp lookout.
                          —UNKNOWN FRIEND

The next night, Tom drew a picture of a skull and crossbones and stuck it on the front door. The following night he put a picture of a coffin on the back door.

The family became all twitchy. I think they would have taken it better if the house had been full of ghosts.

Tom said it was time. Without my knowing, he wrote one final letter:

Someone is going to steal your runaway slave tonight. They've tried to scare you away, but you won't go. I'm a member of the gang, but I've suddenly got religion. I want you to catch them. When I baaa like a sheep, they'll have broken into the hut. Go in there and get them at your leisure.
        —UNKNOWN FRIEND

After breakfast, we sneaked over to the river, got the canoe ready, and checked the raft. When we returned, the family was all excited. They wouldn't tell us why, but Tom told me about the letter so I guessed I knew as much as they did.

That night, Tom awoke me.

"Where's the butter for the getaway lunch?"

"I put it on a piece of cornbread."

"Oh... The cornbread you forgot to pack?"

Tom took one of Aunt Sally's dresses for a disguise for Jim and climbed out the window.

He sent me downstairs to get the bread and butter. Afterwards, I was to meet him and Jim.

Aunt Sally met me at the top of the stairs as I was coming back up—so I quick hid the bread and butter under my hat. When I wouldn't tell her *why* I had been downstairs, she sent me into the living room. I wasn't alone. Fifteen farmers sat in a circle, and every one of them had a gun. I started sweating. Butter ran down my face in globs.

When Sally came into the room, one of the farmers had just said, "I'm going to get in the hut. When they come to steal the slave, I'm going to shoot them."

Aunt Sally saw the globs of melted butter running down my face and shrieked, "He's got brain fever! His brains are oozing out!"

When everyone discovered it was butter, Sally said I should have told her I was hungry. She sent me upstairs, so I climbed on down the lightning rod and met Tom and Jim, already "dressed," in the hut. I told Tom about the house full of men.

"Get ready," Tom said. "When we get a safe distance, you *baaa* like a sheep."

Suddenly we heard the tramping of feet and men's voices outside the hut.

We hit the hole and crawled into the lean-to. We heard the men bust into the hut and we all three crawled out and took off running.

"Who's that?" someone yelled.

"Answer, or we'll shoot!"

We didn't answer. Bullets started whizzing past our heads.

"They're running for the river. Unleash the dogs!"

When we heard the dogs, we jumped into the bushes. The dogs knew all three of us. We petted them. One of the hounds got the scent of a raccoon and then all the hounds took off after it. The men followed, thinking the raccoon was *us*.

When we made it safely back to the raft, I said, "Jim, you won't ever be a slave again. I promise."

Jim was happy, but I swear if I didn't think Tom was the happiest of all. His plan had worked, but more than that, *he'd been shot in the leg!* Jim tried to stop the blood with an old shirt, but it was of little use.

"We've got to get out of here," Tom said.

"Not with you bleeding like that," Jim answered. He turned to me. "Go fetch him a doctor, child."

"Jim, you're going to get caught," Tom said. "Let's go."

"My freedom isn't worth your life," Jim said.

Jim said he'd hide in the bushes when the doctor came. Then he ordered me to get help, so I hurried to bring a doctor. The last words Jim said before I left were: "After we know Tom is safe, I'll get my freedom."

CHAPTER SIXTEEN

Doctoring –
A Hero's Welcome – Freedom

I liked the doctor. He was old, nice, fatherly.

"How did it happen, again?" he asked.

I retold the story. "We'd been hunting and we didn't unload our guns properly. In his sleep my brother rolled over and hit his gun. The gun went off, shooting him in the leg."

He looked at me as if he didn't quite believe me.

I thought our canoe was of good size, but the doctor said only one person could ride safely. I gave him directions and waited on the riverbank. Sometime during the night I fell asleep, for when I opened my eyes the sun had risen.

I saw no sign of the canoe. I hurried to the doctor's house and was told the doctor had been called away during the night and had not yet returned.

I started to hurry back, when a voice took me by surprise. "Where have *you* been?"

I turned, and saw Uncle Silas.

"Your aunt's been so upset for you and your brother."

"She shouldn't have been," I said. "We heard the men and the dogs last night and followed them, but they outran us. When we got to the river, we heard the dogs on the other side. We went across, got tired, and slept. Sid's at the post office."

"We'll go to the post office."

As I suspected, we didn't find Tom at the post office. Uncle Silas grew tired and took me back home with him. "Your brother will find his own way," he said.

When we arrived, neighbors crowded inside the house. A body couldn't believe the stories being told about the escaped slave.

"What creature would scribble all those sick love poems on a wall?"

"Look at that ladder of rags. He was in a

one-story hut. What did he expect to climb?"

"Those knife saws!"

"That's a week's worth for six men."

"That straw dummy he left in his own bed."

"Silas's shirt, covered in bloody writing, in an African language."

"I'd love to know what it said!"

"All those stolen items!"

"The dogs couldn't track them."

"You'd think they were a band of spirits!"

"They just disappeared!"

After everyone had gone home, Aunt Sally asked about the night before. I told her we heard the shots, slid down the lightning rod to learn of what the fuss was about, and then picked up with the same story I'd told Uncle Silas.

By supper, Tom still hadn't shown up. Uncle Silas made another trip to town. He came back alone.

Aunt Sally tucked me in bed. She hugged on me and treated me as her own child. She talked about Tom, only she called him "Sid."

"I'm going to leave the doors and windows unlocked tonight," Aunt Sally said. "I would hope you wouldn't leave and do that to me again."

I worried about Tom all night, but after what

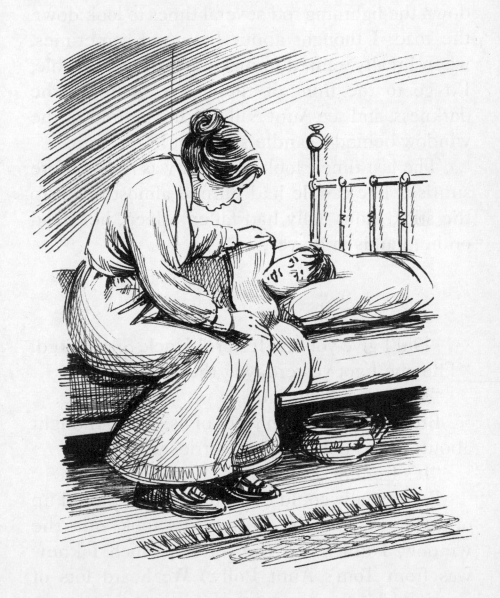

Aunt Sally had said, how could I leave? I did climb
down the lightning rod several times to look down
the road. I thought about Jim. And sometimes,
when I really wanted to make myself feel terrible,
I'd go to the front of the house, stand in the
darkness, and see Aunt Sally sitting in front of the
window behind a candle she kept lit for Tom.

The last time I looked at her was right before
sunrise. The candle had burned almost down to
the stick. Aunt Sally had fallen asleep, her head
on her hands in prayer.

"Did I give you the letter?" Uncle Silas asked.
"The one I got yesterday at the post office?"

"No," said Aunt Sally.

Breakfast sat cold in front of us. We all thought
about Tom. I doubled my worries with Jim.

"It's from St. Petersburg. From Sis."

Before Sally could open it, a wagon pulled up
outside. (When she turned to look out the
window, I quick hid the letter—which I knew
was from Tom's Aunt Polly.) We heard lots of
voices and hurried out.

Outside stood the doctor's wagon, with Jim in the back. Jim still wore Aunt Sally's dress. Tom Sawyer lay on a mattress.

"He's dead!" Aunt Sally cried.

Tom turned his head.

"He's alive!"

They carried Tom into the house. I stayed outside, looking at Jim. I saw his eyes watering.

He didn't act like he knew me. When *my* eyes started to water, he gave me a quick glance. In my own head, I heard his voice: *You be strong, honey.* How many times had he told me that?

Some of the men wanted to hang Jim. Others said that wouldn't solve anything. The men treated Jim awful bad. Jim didn't fight back. He didn't say a word.

You be strong, honey, I thought.

They took Jim back to the hut. They put him in his clothes. They chained him with a chain around each ankle, wrist, and finally his neck. They bolted the chains to the wall.

"Feed him only bread and water," they ordered.

"If his owner doesn't come, we'll sell him at auction."

Then a voice rang out. "Don't be any rougher on him than you have to."

All eyes turned towards the doctor. He'd come from the house where he'd been tending to Tom.

"The boy went into shock right after I got there. When I mumbled aloud, 'I need somebody to help me,' this slave came out of the brush. He had no plan on running. When they tied his arms, he said only one thing—'Is that boy

going to be well?' You can't put a price on a slave like that, much less a man."

The crowd began to soften, but they still kept Jim chained and fed him nothing more.

I slept outside that night. Jim didn't want to talk. A few times I heard him cry. I lay with my head against the hut.

Next morning, I slipped into Tom's room. Aunt Sally appeared at the door and whispered, "We can all be happy now."

Tom opened his eyes. "I'm home? Where's the raft?"

"It's all right," I said.

"And Jim?"

"The same." I didn't know what else to say. Aunt Sally couldn't know that we knew Jim.

"We did it!" Tom exclaimed.

Before I could stop him, Tom went on to tell the whole story, the whole truth of it. Aunt Sally at first couldn't believe Tom's words and then her anger took over.

"And Jim's free!" Tom said.

"The runaway slave?" Aunt Sally asked. "No. He's loaded down with chains eating bread and water until he's claimed or sold."

"That isn't right!" Tom screamed. He sat up in bed. "He's a *free* man. Miss Watson died two months ago. She set him free in her Will."

"Why didn't you tell us?" Aunt Sally asked. "Why did you want to set a *free* man *free?*"

"For the adventure!" Tom said. Then he looked up and gasped, "*Aunt Polly?*"

I turned around. There stood Tom's Aunt Polly. Aunt Sally jumped for her sis. I jumped under the bed.

"Tom," said Aunt Polly, "when you get well, I'm going to beat you back to being ill. And Huck Finn, you get out from under that bed."

Aunt Polly told us that Jim was indeed free. He'd already been free *two whole months.*

I hoped that when Aunt Polly beat Tom back to being ill, she invited me to assist.

When I went outside, Jim was out of his chains and eating real food.

He walked over to me. He walked like a free man—tall, straight, proud.

"Honey, how's Tom?"

I took Jim upstairs. Tom gave Jim $40 for being such a good sport.

"This will go towards buying my family," Jim said. He was happy to get the money, but it didn't make me feel any better thinking about what we'd put him through.

"We can go out west," Tom said.

"Sounds fine to me," I said. "But I don't have any money. I'm sure Pap's gotten it all."

"No," Tom said. "Judge Thatcher's still holding your money."

"Your Pap isn't coming back, child," Jim said. "You remember that floating house? Remember the dead man I wouldn't let you see? That dead man was your Pap."

It's been a few weeks now. Tom's well. He wears his bullet around his neck on a string. After writing this book, I've decided I'll probably never write another one. It's too much work.

I think I'm going out west.

Aunt Sally wants to adopt me. She says she'll make me civilized.

I'd rather not.

I've been there before.

THE END

MARK TWAIN

Mark Twain's real name was Samuel Langhorne Clemens. He was born in 1835, just as Halley's Comet blazed through the sky. He grew up in Hannibal, Missouri, where he rafted on the river and had an adventurous young life.

When his father died, young Samuel went to work as a typesetter for a newspaper. He also traveled across America, working at a variety of jobs—from miner to soldier to riverboat pilot.

His own love of words and storytelling led him to become a writer. He took his pen name, Mark Twain, from a riverboat term which meant "two fathoms deep." His witty stories became very popular. In 1876, *The Adventures of Tom Sawyer* was published, which introduced America (and the world) to Tom Sawyer and Huck Finn. He published several more famous stories, such as *The Prince and the Pauper* (1882), and *A Connecticut Yankee in King Arthur's Court* (1889), but it was *The Adventures of Huckleberry Finn* (1885) which proved to be his biggest success. It is considered one of the best American novels.

Twain died in 1910, just as Halley's Comet blazed again through the sky.

Moby Dick

HERMAN MELVILLE

CONDENSED AND ADAPTED BY
W.T. ROBINSON

ILLUSTRATED BY
JERRY DILLINGHAM

CONTENTS

ISHMAEL — that's me, the teller of this tale,
a young man who goes to sea on a whaling ship

PETER COFFIN — the innkeeper of
The Spouter Inn

QUEEQUEG — a tattooed South Sea native,
an expert harpooner, my good friend

PELEG AND CAPTAIN BILDAD — the
owners of our ship, the *Pequod*

CAPTAIN AHAB — a dark sea captain with
one cry— "Have ye seen the White Whale?"

STARBUCK — chief mate on the *Pequod*,
a good man with a wise heart

STUBB — second mate, a cheery sailor who smokes a pipe

FLASK — third mate, a short, tough sailor

TASHTEGO — a long, lean American Indian, Stubb's harpooner

DAGGOO — a giant African, Flask's harpooner

FEDALLAH — a mysterious man with a small band of nameless crewmen, Ahab's harpooner and advisor

Ships we meet on our long sail at sea:
JEROBOAM
SAMUEL ENDERBY
BACHELOR
RACHEL
DELIGHT

Moby Dick

CHAPTER ONE

A New Freedom

Call me Ishmael. A few years ago, with no money in my wallet and nothing interesting to do on shore, I thought I would sail around a little on the watery part of the world. There is something mystical about being on the water, free of the land. I had been to sea many times before, but never to hunt whales. I don't know why, but this just seemed what I had to do this time. I would find a whaling ship and see if I could join the crew. The thrill of hunting the huge monster of the ocean and sailing the distant seas began to fill my mind. This was going to be exciting!

So, on a cold December morning, I stuffed a

shirt or two into an old suitcase and left my home for New Bedford, Massachusetts. From there I could take a ferry to Nantucket where I would get on a whaling ship.

I arrived in New Bedford on a cold, wet night. I could smell the ocean's salty air as I walked the New Bedford streets in search of a bed for the night. As I neared the waterfront, I saw a sign swinging in the wind that read *The Spouter Inn* – Peter Coffin. I liked the name of the place since I would be looking for whale spouts at sea. The owner's last name gave me a little shiver up my spine, but I would worry about that later. I went inside.

On one wall hung a painting of a huge whale about to attack a sinking ship. On another wall I saw a collection of old, rusted whaling spears, called harpoons, which are used to kill the giant fish. There were sailors sitting around carving things from the bones and teeth of whales.

Mr. Coffin told me he had no empty beds. "But wait," he said, "you can share a bed with a harpooner. If you are goin' whalin' you best get used to that sort of thing." I told him I never liked to sleep two to a bed. But I was too cold and

hungry to argue. I said I would give it a try.

At last, a good hot supper of meat, potatoes, and dumplings was served. "When will I meet this harpooner?" I asked the landlord. "What time does he go to bed?"

"Oh, you won't be seein' him for a long time yet, lad," Coffin said with a grin. "He's somewhere in town sellin' those shrunken heads he picks up in the South Sea islands."

Shrunken heads? I thought. Now I was too afraid to go to bed and too tired to stay awake. Finally, the landlord calmed me down a little and showed me to my room. Placing a candle on an old sea chest next to the bed, he wished me sweet dreams and left.

All I could think about was this harpooner and what sort of a night it was going to be. Gathering enough courage to get into bed, I put myself in God's care for the night. Whether that mattress was stuffed with corn cobs or broken dishes, I don't know, but I rolled and tossed a lot and could not sleep for a long time. I had finally slipped off into a light doze when I heard some heavy footsteps in the hall. A ray of light came into the room from under the door.

I lay perfectly still, waiting to see what would happen. The stranger entered the room, holding a light in one hand and a terrible shrunken head in the other. Good heavens! What a sight! His face was a dark purplish-yellow color, and there were tattoos all over his face and body. His hair was tied up in a knot on top of his head.

After he placed his candle on the floor, he pulled something out of a big bag in the corner of the room. It looked like a tomahawk! I was scared, but I tried to lie still and remember that a man who is ugly on the outside can still be good on the inside. Just as I had begun to calm down a little, this huge, dark savage took a wooden black doll from within his coat. Then he lit a small fire from some wood chips and began praying a strange prayer. Finally, he blew out his candle and jumped into bed. I screamed out in fear!

"Who-ee debel you?" the dark stranger asked. "Speakee to me! You no speakee—I killee!"

"Save me! Save me, landlord!" I shouted. "Please help me!"

I heard some footsteps in the hall. When the landlord came into the room, I leaped from my bed and ran up to him.

"Don't be afraid," he said, grinning at me. "Queequeg here wouldn't harm a hair on your head."

The landlord spoke to Queequeg, telling him we were going to "sleepee" together, and everything would be fine. And he was right. Queequeg climbed quietly into bed. He no longer seemed so strange. Maybe he had been as afraid of me as I of him. He was peaceful and calm now as he drifted off to sleep. I rolled over and never slept better in my life.

The sun was just coming up when I awoke the next morning. Queequeg was snoring loudly. I looked at the colorful tattoos that covered his body. What an odd sight the first thing in the morning! I shook him gently, for I could not get out of bed until he awoke and moved—no luck. "Queequeg!"—more snores. Here I was, trapped next to a savage with a tomahawk at his side! "Queequeg, Queequeg, wake up!"

At last, with some grunts and groans, he got up, put on a tall hat and boots, and then began to wash and shave. But where was his razor? That was soon answered when he picked up his harpoon. Moving to a bit of mirror against the wall, he began to scrape (or should I say *harpoon*?) his cheeks. How sharp that harpoon must be!

After his shaving and bathing were complete, Queequeg finished dressing. Holding his harpoon before him as though he were leading a band, he proudly marched out of the room.

I quickly dressed and went downstairs to get some breakfast. Seated at the table were people such as I had never seen. There were whaling sailors of all kinds. I could see the effects of sun and salt-sea air on their tanned, cracked faces. They were a shaggy lot. There were chief mates, second mates, third mates, sea carpenters, barrel makers, blacksmiths, harpooners, cooks, and common deckhands. I joined the group just as a loud "Grub ho!" from the landlord told me that breakfast was on its way.

Queequeg sat at the head of the table, cool as an icicle. His manners were a bit strange, however. He had brought his harpoon to breakfast and began using it to reach across the length of the table to spear the beefsteaks. He ate none of the hot rolls, nor did he drink the hot coffee. He ate only the rarest of the steak. When he had enough, he sat back to relax and smoke his tomahawk, which to my surprise turned out to be his pipe.

When breakfast was over, I decided to take a walk around the town. Both the rich and the poor filled the streets. Sailors from all parts of the world, dressed in every type of clothing, walked side by side with wealthy visitors from the nearby states of Vermont and New Hampshire. It was a Sunday, and I heard a preacher telling about Jonah and the Whale. That was not what I wanted to hear just before I went on my whale hunt!

CHAPTER TWO

A New Friend

When I returned to *The Spouter Inn*, I found Queequeg alone, quietly humming a tune and whittling the face of the wooden doll he called Yojo. I watched him for awhile. There was a kindness in his eyes which must have come from inside his soul. He had a proud look. I thought that he must be a man of honesty and courage.

We talked a little, and I offered to help him understand a book he had taken off the shelf. He seemed thankful for my kindness and offered me a smoke. As we passed the pipe back and forth in the warmth of the small fire burning in our room, a change took place in our hearts. When our

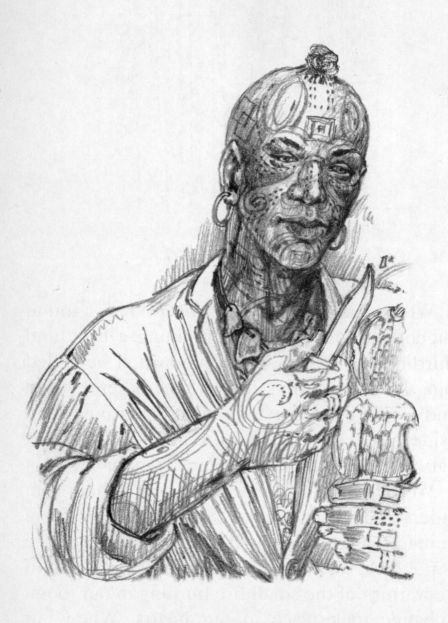

smoke was finished, Queequeg pressed his forehead to mine and told me that we were now to be lifetime friends. He even said he would die for me if ever he had to.

The following morning it was time to find a ferry to Nantucket. I paid the bill for the stay at the inn and borrowed a wheelbarrow into which we loaded our things. The landlord was surprised to see the new friendship between Queequeg and me as he watched us heading off together for the dock.

We paid for our trip on the *Moss*, a small ship headed for Nantucket, and loaded our things on board. The breeze filled the small ship's sails. The salt air licked against my face. My thoughts turned to the sea. I took one last look at the land behind us.

CHAPTER THREE

The Pequod

It was nearly dark when we reached Nantucket. What a place it was—a small wind-blown island with no trees and very few plants. The Indians discovered the island many years ago. Then came the white men who first sailed from its shore in search of fish. Now, men sailed to all corners of the world from this tiny seaport. Mr. Coffin had told us that his cousin, Hosea Hussey, owned an inn called *The Try Pots*. After wandering around and getting lost several times, we finally found the place. Mr. Hussey's wife served us some delicious soup of clams and codfish. I was glad to see that Queequeg didn't

try to harpoon the small pieces of fish in the soup as he had speared the steaks earlier in the day. After supper, we went upstairs to bed. Tomorrow we would find a ship and prepare to go on a great adventure.

I woke early, and, while Queequeg was still having his morning prayers with Yojo, I found my way down to the docks. There were several whaling ships. One caught my eye. It was named *Pequod*. Although its decks were old and battered, the three tall poles, called masts, which held the sails, stood tall and straight. Spying a small tent near the docked ship, I peeked inside.

"Are you the captain of the *Pequod*?" I asked the man seated in the tent.

"I am an owner of the ship ye name," the old sailor answered in a rough voice. "Who wants to know?"

"My name is Ishmael. I and a friend of mine want to sign up to go hunting whales on your ship."

"Well, my name is Peleg, and what do ye know about whaling, young lad?" the owner asked.

"I don't know much," I confessed. "But I've worked on other kinds of ships, and I want to learn. Please give me a try."

Peleg took me to the other owner of the ship, Captain Bildad. They asked me more questions and finally signed me on. My pay would be low, and the work would be hard and dangerous.

"Captain Peleg," I said, "I have a friend who wants to go, too. Shall I bring him down tomorrow?"

"Fine," said Peleg. "Bring him along, and we'll have a look at him. Has he ever hunted whales?"

"Killed more whales than I can count, Captain Peleg."

After signing the papers, I wanted to meet the man who would sail as captain of the ship. Peleg and Bildad told me I would meet him later. They told me that he could be a good man and a terrible one at the same time. His name was Ahab, and he had lost a leg fighting a whale. As I walked away, I thought about this strange Captain Ahab. A man with a good side and a bad side could be hard to work for.

When I arrived back at the inn that evening, Mrs. Hussey told me that Queequeg had spent the whole day in the room praying. I didn't disturb him. I was sure we would need all the

prayers we could get. I quietly crawled into bed and was soon asleep.

The next morning, we ate a huge breakfast of fish soups of all kinds. When we were full, we packed our bags and headed out to get on the *Pequod*, picking our teeth with fish bones along the way.

As we were walking along the dock toward the ship, Captain Peleg shouted at us from his tent saying I had not told him my friend was a wild-looking savage. I argued strongly for my tattooed friend. I said that we were all God's children and that they would find Queequeg a man they could trust. They still made fun of Queequeg, even his name.

"Quohog, Hedgehog, or whatever your name is, did ye ever stand at the head of a whaleboat? Did ye ever spear a fish?" cried Peleg.

Without saying a word—but with a wild gleam in his eye—Queequeg jumped over the ship's rails and into one of the small whaleboats hanging on the side. Then, raising his harpoon, he cried out something like this:

"Cap'ain, you see him small drop oil on water far away over dere? Well, sposee him a whale's eye den!" And taking sharp aim at it, he threw

the harpoon right past Bildad's head and hit the shining oil spot square in the center.

"Now," said Queequeg, quietly pulling in the line of the harpoon, "sposee him tar spot whalee eye. Well, dat whale dead!"

When they saw Queequeg's skill, the owners said he could join the crew. I was proud of my friend who, though he could not write, made his mark on the papers we were asked to sign. I noticed that it was the same mark as one of the tattoos on his arm. It had been a good morning. Things were looking bright.

A day or two passed, and there was a lot of activity onboard the *Pequod* as it was loaded for the three-year trip. New sails were brought aboard, and old sails were being mended. Coils of rope, harpoons, food, water, empty barrels to store the whale oil, and every other thing you could imagine were stored below the ship's decks. But we had still not seen that strange Ahab.

With no captain to direct things, I was glad to hear one of the sailors say that our chief mate was bustling around. "Halloa! Starbuck's on the move," said the sailor. "He's a lively chief, he.

A good man and a religious one."

By now the sun was high in the sky. The crew began to climb aboard the ship. Around noon, when the final list of duties was complete, the *Pequod* was pushed away from the dock. At last the anchor was pulled up, the wind began to fill the sails, and off we glided. My heart was beating like a drum. What a Christmas day this was! My dream was coming true. My new adventure on the sea had begun. Bring on the whales!

CHAPTER FOUR

Merry Christmas

It was a cold Christmas. As the day turned into night, we found ourselves upon a wintry ocean. A freezing spray wrapped us in ice. Like the white ivory tusks of some huge elephant, giant, curving icicles hung from the ship's rails.

Once we had reached a distance from shore, the two owners' work was done. A smaller boat, which had followed us out from Nantucket, pulled alongside to take Bildad and Peleg back to shore. The old sailors said their good-byes and wished us a safe journey.

"God bless ye, and keep ye, men," said Bildad. "I hope ye have fine weather. Don't

forget thy prayers. Be careful in the hunt, mates. Watch that leak in the molasses jug…" On and on he went, until Peleg finally told him it was past time to go. I could see that these old sailors missed going to sea and were putting off returning to land as long as they could. As they climbed into the boat headed back to shore, there were tears in the eyes of the two tough whale hunters.

The smaller boat slowly disappeared from sight. A screaming bird flew over us. We gave three cheers and slid into the lonely Atlantic seas.

CHAPTER FIVE

Shipmates

Several days passed with not a sign of Captain Ahab. I did, however, meet the others of our crew. The chief mate of the *Pequod* was Starbuck, a native of Nantucket and a good person. He was a tall, slender man, but hard as nails. The rest of the men looked up to him because he was calm and steady. He was only thirty, but he seemed older. Perhaps the deaths of his father and brother during past whaling trips made him that way. He had great courage, but he was also very careful. He knew the dangers of hunting giant whales.

Stubb, the second mate, was from Cape Cod,

Massachusetts. He was happy and carefree and I was told he could be heard humming a tune right in the middle of a battle with a whale. Stubb had a pipe in his mouth all of the time. He kept a whole row of pipes full and ready to go.

The third mate was Flask, another Massachusetts native—a short, chubby young fellow, always ready for a fight with a whale. It was said he would toy with a whale as if it were just a big mouse. Flask was tough and steady.

Now, these three mates, Starbuck, Stubb, and Flask, were very important men. They were each in charge of a whaleboat and its crew. These whaleboats were lowered over the sides of the main ship when whales were sighted. The whaleboat crews were made up of the men who pulled the oars, and the harpooner. When the time came to attack and kill a whale, the harpooner's skill with his spear usually decided who won the battle. The men in each crew trusted one another like brothers.

Starbuck had chosen Queequeg for his harpooner. You have already heard about him. Next was Tashtego, a full-blooded Massachusetts Indian, known for his bravery and daring. Tashtego was long and lean and strong as a steel wire. Tashtego was Stubb's harpooner. The third harpooner was Daggoo, a gigantic, coal-black African. With two hoop earrings and a height of six feet and five inches, he was quite a sight next to little Flask, the mate with whom he worked.

There was another whaleboat crew on the *Pequod*, though nothing was known about them. One night before we sailed, a crew had slipped on board like shadows and disappeared into the area of Ahab's cabin. They were more like ghosts than men. The gossip was that they were Ahab's personal crew, led by a strange man named Fedallah.

The rest of the crew came in all shapes, sizes, and colors—from all over the world, especially islands. Most of the crew had spent their whole lives on the sea and were expert whalemen. Many had hidden aboard ships that had been passing their islands, and they had never returned. The whaling ship became their home, their own little island.

CHAPTER SIX

Ahab

While Ahab remained hidden in his cabin below the deck, the three mates ran the ship. Starbuck, Stubb, and Flask took their turns at keeping watch for whales as we fought our way south through a freezing wind. But as we sailed farther south, the weather began to turn warmer.

It was on a cloudy morning just before noon that Ahab finally appeared. I was on deck at the back of the ship. I looked over my shoulder and then looked again. Sure enough, there he stood. Shivers ran all through me. His skin was a dark, bronze color, and his head was a mass of long, gray hair. Winding out of his hair and right down one side of his face and neck was an ugly white scar.

I stared at this face for several moments, unable to move my eyes from it. It was only after I began to believe what I saw that I noticed the rest of him. As my eyes ran down his body, I saw that leg I had already heard about. A slender, white stump stuck out from one of Ahab's trouser legs. It was a piece of ivory taken from a whale's jaw. A hole had been drilled on each side of the ship's deck to match the size of the leg's bottom tip. Ahab's false leg rested in one of those holes as he stood there like a statue, his eyes never leaving the open seas ahead of us.

Before long, this strange-looking man turned away and disappeared into his cabin. It was several days before we would see him again, but as the days became less gloomy he came on deck more often. Still, he said not a word to the crew.

The days had become sunnier, and the night skies twinkled with a million stars. The waves caught the light from the heavens, and the water was a flashing, glittering carpet of blue and silver stretching before us.

Ahab spent some time on deck nearly every

day, and most nights. The crew could hear the tapping and thumping of that ivory leg as he paced back and forth above their bunks. We began to wonder when he got any sleep, or if he slept at all.

One night, Stubb asked him to return to his cabin so the rest of us could get some sleep. Ahab became angry, called him a dog, and charged at him with a most terrible look in his eyes. Poor Stubb was scared to death and ran back to his cabin. Our captain was full of a restless anger of some kind. I thought it might be a hatred toward the whale that had chewed his leg off.

CHAPTER SEVEN

A *Short Science Lesson*

Before we get much deeper into our chase for the whale, I should give you a few facts about this huge beast. You need to know a little bit about what to expect, for we are coming into the whale's neighborhood now.

First, let me say that I do not agree with those scientists who call the whale a mammal. I cannot see how anything that spends its entire life in the water could be anything but a fish. And even the Bible says that the creature that swallowed Jonah was a "great fish."

I do agree that there are some differences between the whale and other fish. First, the whale

has lungs and warm blood. This means he must come to the surface of the water to fill his lungs with air and to control his temperature. When he rises to the surface to take a breath, he spits out the old air and takes in new—just like we human beings inhale and exhale through our nose and mouth. But the whale does it a little differently. He has a blowhole located in the center of his forehead (except for the Sperm whale, whose blowhole is at the front and to its left). When the air blows through this hole it comes out with such force that it creates a burst of air and water, or spout. This misty spout is the first thing a whale hunter looks for as he stands watch on the deck, and it is the reason for the famous shout:

"There she blows!"

I'll mention just one more thing that one notices about whales—the broad tail. All the other fish have up-and-down (or vertical) tails. But the whale's tail lies flat. So, if you see a spouting fish with a huge, flat tail, you will have spotted a whale.

Now, among these warm-blooded, air-breathing, spouting, flat-tailed fishes, there are many types. Of these, the *Sperm Whale, Humpbacked Whale, Razor Back Whale,* and *Right Whale*

are the largest and most valuable for the quality and amount of oil they contain. And of this group, the Sperm whale is the king of the fishes, just as the lion is king of the beasts. He is the hardest thing to kill, but the tons of valuable oil that come from his body make hunting him worth the danger. His oil lights the lamps around the world. The Sperm whale is also the only whale from which we get spermaceti. This precious substance is used to make expensive perfumes.

Before ending this little science lesson, I should give you some idea about the size of the whale. Many whales grow to be over ninety feet in length, and old sailors would tell you they have seen great creatures which would measure more than that! The largest of the Sperm whales weigh over ninety tons! I could go on with facts and stories, but you shall learn more about these marvelous fish as the journey continues.

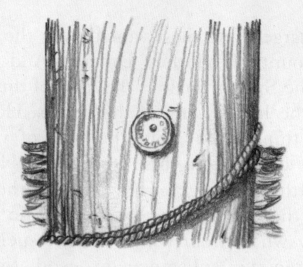

CHAPTER EIGHT

The Gold Doubloon

One evening, after pacing back and forth all day, Ahab suddenly stopped. He put his ivory leg into its hole on the deck and ordered Starbuck to send everybody to the rear of the ship's deck.

"Send everybody aft," shouted Ahab. "Men up there on the masts, come down!"

When the entire crew was in front of him, Ahab stared at them with a gleam in his eyes.

"What do ye do when ye see a whale, men?" he cried.

"Sing out for him!" shouted the crew.

"Good!" cried Ahab, with a wild sound in his voice. "And what d'ye do next, men?"

"Lower the whaleboats away, and go after him!"
"And what tune d'ye sing as ye pull the oars?"
"*A dead whale or a sunk boat!*"
"Look! Do ye see this Spanish ounce of gold? It is a sixteen-dollar piece, men, a doubloon. Do ye see it? Mr. Starbuck, hand me that yonder hammer."

While the chief mate was getting the hammer, Ahab was slowly rubbing the gold piece against his jacket, humming a strange sound that seemed to come from deep inside him. Starbuck returned and handed our captain the hammer. He then nailed the gold coin to the mast. Turning to face us he cried out:

"Whoever finds me a White Whale with a wrinkled head and a crooked jaw… Whoever first sights that White Whale with three holes in his right fin… Whoever of ye boys that first finds me that same White Whale… *he* shall have this gold piece!"

"Hurray! Hurray!" cried the seamen.

"It's a White Whale, I say," repeated Ahab, as he threw down the hammer. "A White Whale! Peel your eyes for him! Look sharp! If ye see no more than a bubble, sing out!"

"Captain Ahab," said Tashtego, "that White Whale must be the one called Moby Dick."

"Moby Dick?" shouted Ahab. "Do ye know the White Whale then, Tash?"

"And does he have a different sort of spout?" asked Daggoo.

"And does he have many harpoon on him, too, Captain?" cried Queequeg.

"Aye, harpoons all in him, Queequeg. Yes, Daggoo, his spout is a big one, and white as snow. Death and devils, men. It is Moby Dick ye have spoken of—Moby Dick!"

"Captain Ahab," said Starbuck, "I have heard of Moby Dick. But was it this Moby Dick that took off thy leg?"

"Who told you that?" cried Ahab. "Aye, Starbuck, it was Moby Dick that caused this dead stump I stand on now. Yes," he shouted bitterly, sounding like some wounded animal, "it was that cursed whale and I'll chase him around every ocean in the world before I'm done!"

Starbuck spoke up. "I am willing to chase this White Whale to the death if it means money in our pockets, but there will be little reward if all we are after is revenge upon a dumb animal. Such a hunt would be crazy and against the laws of God. Thou art not asking for our skill, Captain Ahab. Thou art asking for our lives."

Ahab went on screaming about his hatred for Moby Dick. He was like a crazy man who would

listen to no one. The three mates backed away from him as they saw that nothing would calm the storm inside Ahab's dark soul. Starbuck's face was white as chalk. He shivered and turned away. "God keep me! God keep us all!" murmured Starbuck to himself.

But Ahab did not hear him. He had already left to return to his cabin, the white ivory peg tapping, tapping, tapping across the ship's deck. A gray fog crept over the ship, but the gold doubloon still shone brightly on the mast.

CHAPTER NINE

Moby Dick

The days and weeks passed. The wind filled our sails and pulled our ship across miles and miles of the world's great oceans. I stayed busy with my sailor's tasks. There was always something to be done. As I worked with the others, whether it was scrubbing decks, mending nets, or keeping watch for whales, I kept my ears open to the stories they told. I was most interested in the tales about Moby Dick.

Much of what I heard seemed to be nothing but gossip and rumors. At the same time, some of the things must have been true because more than one sailor often repeated the same facts.

For instance, I was told that Moby Dick was larger than even the largest Sperm whales anyone had ever seen. He had a white, wrinkled forehead and a crooked lower jaw. And, according to most accounts, he carried in his side several harpoons left there by past efforts to catch him. Whether it was because of these harpoons sticking in him, or whether it was just Moby Dick's own nature, I do not know, but every sailor swore he was an angry, vicious murderer who would attack the ships and men hunting him.

These same sailors, however, also said there was a strange beauty and mystery about him. Some even said that Moby Dick had been sighted in two different oceans at the same time. It was almost as though there were things both real and unreal about him—things both good and evil. But everybody agreed on one thing: It was this whale, this Moby Dick, that had attacked Captain Ahab and chewed his leg from him.

These stories that I heard during my days stayed with me into my nights. I tossed and turned and could not sleep.

CHAPTER TEN

Our First Whale

The weeks turned into months, and still we had seen no whales. We sailed through storms that ripped at our sails and tossed our ship on waves as tall as a house. There were times when I was sure we would be swamped with water or thrown over the side. Then, there were other days when the wind was so calm that there was barely enough in the sails to move us along. I hoped and prayed that Captain Ahab knew where we were and where the whales were.

On one of those calm days, I was on deck with Queequeg helping to weave a mat. The sky was completely clouded over, and the air was hot and damp. There we were weaving away, drawing the straw in and out, in and out, lost in a daydream—when a strange, musical cry shook me.

"There she blows! She blows! There she blows! About two miles! A whole school of 'em!" Tashtego called from his lookout watch on top of the mast.

All at once, the whole ship jumped into action. Tashtego had spotted whales!

My heart was racing. My first whale! I rushed to the side of the ship along with the others. This was the moment I had been waiting for!

At Ahab's command, the mates, along with their harpooners and crews, leaped to the rails, ready to lower their whaleboats into the water. The rest of the crew ran in all directions. Each harpooner had grabbed his spear and looked as though he could not wait to begin the chase.

Suddenly, all eyes left the whales and stared at Ahab. He was surrounded by five dark phantoms that seemed to have come out of the air. They flitted to the other side of the deck and, without a sound, lowered a boat that hung there. The rest of us had thought this was a spare boat, but we now saw that it was for Ahab.

A tall, dark figure stood in the front of the boat. He was dressed all in black, and his white hair was twisted and coiled up into a white turban.

This was Ahab's private crew. Ahab must have hidden them in his cabin until just the right time. We had heard whispers about this phantom crew. Now they were above decks for the first time and leaping into Ahab's boat.

While the rest of us were still trying to understand what was happening, Ahab cried out to the dark figure standing in the harpooner's position at the front of his boat, "All ready there, Fedallah?"

"Ready," said Fedallah. His voice sounded like a hiss.

"Lower away then," shouted Ahab. "Lower the boats, I say!"

The thunder in Ahab's voice caused the crews to spring over the ship's side into the tossing boats. Ahab's strange crew appeared in their boat, coming around the other end of the ship. Ahab stood at the rear. Fedallah was perched in front, and the four other mysterious men pulled at the oars.

We stared for a moment at the eerie crew. Starbuck wondered whether we should join this crew of mysterious devils. Finally, carefree Stubb convinced him that even devils could kill a whale, and all four boats began the chase.

I was on Starbuck's crew. We pulled on the oars until we thought our backs would break. The waves tossed us like toothpicks as we struggled to make our way in the direction of the whale spouts.

"Pull harder! Faster to the whale! Break your backs, you dogs!" cried Ahab.

I had never in my life been through anything like this. My back and neck ached, and I thought I could pull no harder on the oars without ripping my arms off. The waves curled and licked around us as we followed the spouts of mist coming from the whales. Then the clouds grew darker, and we lost sight of the other boats. The salty spray rushed into my eyes until they burned like fire. The storm grew worse, and the mist turned into a thick fog.

I could hear the voices of the other mates shouting at their crews to row harder and fight on through the waves. The voices became fainter as the boats were pulled further apart. Even the *Pequod* had disappeared from sight.

"Hang on, men," whispered Starbuck. "There is still time to kill a fish before the rain comes. There's white water again! Jump! Spring! Stand up, Queequeg!"

There was a moment of silence. Then: "That's his hump. There, there, give it to him," ordered Starbuck.

A short, whistling sound filled my ears as Queequeg's harpoon flew through the air. Then, all at once, the whale rose beneath us like an earthquake and a giant wave crashed over us from behind. Our boat was lifted out of the water like a toy. A rush of hot mist shot up from the whale's head as it rolled and tumbled under the boat. The next thing I knew, the whole crew was flying through the air and into the churning water. To make things even worse, the whale had escaped. Queequeg's harpoon had only angered him.

Heads began bobbing to the surface. By some miracle, we were all alive. We began swimming toward our boat, picking up our oars as we went. We tumbled back into the boat, and there we sat, up to our knees in water that had flooded in.

The wind began to howl and the storm roared and snapped around us like a lion. We shouted out, but there was no answer. The sky grew darker with the shadows of night, and still there was no sign of our ship. Starbuck dug around in the waterproof sack tied to the boat and found some dry matches. He lit the boat's lantern and told Queequeg to hold it up like a tiny lighthouse.

By morning, we were running out of hope. The fog still spread over the sea. Suddenly, Queequeg jumped to his feet, holding his hand to his ear. We all heard a faint creaking. Then we saw our ship about to run over us. We jumped overboard just before our boat disappeared under the *Pequod*.

I was the last to be pulled from the sea. I lay on the deck, thanking God to be alive. I learned that Stubb and Flask had harpooned a whale, but they had to cut it loose because of the storm. The strange thing to me was that no one was upset. They acted as though this was all part of the job of whaling. I had great respect for their courage in the face of death.

CHAPTER ELEVEN

The Mysterious Spout

The next day and the next week brought smooth sailing. We had passed by a famous whaling area off the coast of Africa, but not a spout had we seen. On we went toward the tip of Africa and the Cape of Good Hope.

One peaceful and moonlit night a silvery jet rose up far in front of the ship. Fedallah was the first to see it. His weird cry rang out. "There she blows!"

Every sleeping sailor leaped from his bed. Ahab flew from his cabin. The rapid tapping of his dead stump sounded like nails being hammered into a coffin. He ordered a sharp watch, but the mysterious spout was seen no more that night.

Some days later, at the same, silent midnight hour, it returned. Again, all swore they saw it, but as soon as we turned to chase it, it was gone as if it had never been there.

The same thing happened for the next few nights. We could never catch this ghost. It was as if a spirit were tempting us, pulling us toward it.

There are many mysteries in this world that can never be explained. I thought Fedallah might know the meaning of the mysterious spout, but that strange man said nothing.

CHAPTER TWELVE

The Squid

As we entered the Indian Ocean, a gentle, peaceful air settled upon us. The breezes filling our sails made our masts look like three palm trees bending softly back and forth.

One clear, blue morning, Daggoo saw a frightening sight as he kept his watch on the top of the main mast. In the distance, a great white shape rose to the top of the water and shone before our ship like a huge drift of snow. The glistening thing stayed on the surface for a short time, then sank slowly from sight. Silently, it came up again. Daggoo could not be sure what he was seeing. It didn't look like a whale, but could it be Moby Dick?

Again the weird shape went down, but the next time it rose Daggoo screamed, "There! There again! She rises! Right ahead!"

The seamen rushed to their positions on deck like a swarm of bees. Ahab stood on the bow ready to bark his orders and stared in the direction of Daggoo's outstretched arm. As soon as he caught sight of the white hulk, he gave orders to lower all the boats.

The four boats were soon on the water, all pulling toward the object in the water. Suddenly it went down, and just as suddenly came back. For a few moments we forgot about Moby Dick and stared at the most amazing of all the things that hide in the secret seas. A giant, jellylike mass, creamy in color, lay floating on the water. Long arms reached out from its center, curling and twisting like a nest of snakes. It seemed to have no face, or none we could see.

With a low sucking sound it slowly disappeared again. Starbuck, still staring at the boiling water where it had sunk, shrieked with a wild voice, "I would almost rather have seen Moby Dick and fought him than to have seen thee, thou white ghost!"

"What was it, sir?" said Flask.

"The great live squid," said Starbuck quietly. "They say that not many whale hunters who see the beast ever return to tell about it."

But Ahab said nothing. Turning his boat, he returned to the ship. The other boats followed silently behind him.

There are plenty of tales and superstitions about the squid. Some say it is the largest creature in the sea. It is so seldom seen, however, that there are very few facts to pass on. It is true that some whales' bellies have held arms of this monster which were thirty feet long! It is also believed that of all the types of whales, only the Sperm whale eats the squid as his only source of food.

I wasn't sure what to believe about the squid, but what Starbuck had said made me wonder whether any of us would set foot on land again. Queequeg had a happier way of looking at it.

"When you see him squid," he said, sharpening his harpoon to a razor's edge, "then you quick see him Sperm whale."

CHAPTER THIRTEEN

Stubb Kills a Whale

The next day was warm and still. I was keeping watch on top of the masthead while my mind wandered and dreamed of things far away. As I swayed back and forth with the gentle rocking of the mast, I soon became sleepy. The whole crew was lazy on that quiet afternoon.

Suddenly, a bursting of bubbles from the water below me brought me back to life. I was so surprised that I had to grab the sail lines and hang on for dear life. When I got over my shock and looked below, the sight almost took my breath away. Close below me, not more than a hundred yards away, a giant Sperm whale lay rolling in the water. His broad back shone in the sun like a mirror. He looked like a big silver ship. In a split second, our sleepy ship was awake. Cries burst from all three masts. The familiar call, "There she blows!" rang across the decks. Below us, the great fish kept up its lazy rolling. Every so often it sent a sparkling, misty spout into the air.

"Clear away the boats! Prepare to lower!" Ahab cried.

The noise and shouting of the crew must have scared the whale. He began moving slowly away. We paddled our boats as quietly as possible, but as we got near, the monster threw his broad tail forty feet straight up in the air and dove out of sight.

"There he dives!" was the cry. We knew we had nothing to do now but wait for the whale to come to the surface. To my surprise, Stubb sat back and lit his pipe.

After a short time, the whale shot up directly in front of Stubb's boat. Stubb decided that this was his whale to kill. Still puffing on his pipe, Stubb cheered his crew on.

"Give it all you've got, my men! But keep cool. Pull with long, strong strokes but be cool as

cucumbers. Be ready there, Tashtego. Stand up and be ready!"

"Woo-hoo Wa-hee!" screamed the Indian harpooner.

The crew pulled together. They came closer and closer to the whale. When they were nearly on top of him, Stubb shouted, "Give it to him, Tash! Give it to him!"

Tashtego's harpoon sailed through the air straight into the whale. The whale dove, taking the harpoon with it. Finally, after pulling the boat behind it on a wild, crashing ride, the whale slowed. "Haul in! Haul in!" cried Stubb. The crew began pulling the line in, bringing the boat right next to the huge whale. Stubb planted his feet as firmly as he could and threw spear after spear into the whale.

The puffs of steamy mist coming from the whale's spout hole grew smaller. The puffs of smoke from Stubb's pipe seemed to come twice as fast. The battle was nearly over.

The water was a bubbling pool of red foam. Stubb ordered his crew to pull up beside the whale. As the boat came within a few feet of the wounded giant, Stubb drove one last spear deep into the area of its heart. With one last great rush of spray, the whale rolled on its side and lay still in the water.

"He's dead, Mr. Stubb," said Tashtego.

The thrill of the hunt was over, but there was some long, hard work ahead for all of us. Stubb's whale had been killed a long distance from the ship. This made the job of getting the huge fish pulled in even harder.

Ahab's crew had returned to the ship. We tied the other three boats together in a line and began towing our prize to the ship. Eighteen men and thirty-six arms worked together hour after hour, tugging and hauling the great fish toward the ship. Sometimes it seemed as though we moved just an inch at a time.

Darkness came. Lanterns hanging from the *Pequod* guided us. The oarsmen, their backs and arms aching and burning, continued to struggle and pull. Captain Ahab hung a final lantern on the ship's side. His eyes had an empty, hollow look as he stared at the dead whale. Although we had killed a whale, he seemed sad and angry. It was as if he could never be happy until Moby Dick had been killed—that great beast that had

stolen his leg. We could kill a thousand whales, but until the White Whale was dead, Ahab would find no peace.

Unlike Ahab, Stubb was so happy and excited we couldn't get him to calm down. He laughed and made jokes with the crew. He asked the cook to prepare him a feast of whale steak to celebrate the victory. Daggoo leaped over the side and cut a slab of meat from the whale. The cook then made it exactly as Stubb wanted. When he had stuffed himself, Stubb lit his pipe and leaned back in his chair.

Around midnight, we went below decks to our bunks. But we didn't sleep much. Stubb was not the only one that night to have a late bite of whale meat.

Thousands of sharks began to circle the ship and move in for their own feast. You could hear their tails smack and snap against the ship's sides. They were fighting each other for a place at their own supper table. When the sharks finally left, I closed my eyes and drifted off to sleep. As it turned out, I would need all the rest I could get. There was still a lot of work ahead before there would be whale oil in our barrels.

CHAPTER FOURTEEN

Cutting Up

The following day was Sunday. Back on land, shops and factories were closed and people were in church. Things were quite different on a whaling ship if a huge whale hung there waiting to be cut up. No, there would be no rest on this Sunday.

As I said before, the reason men hunt whales is to get the oil from their bodies. Most of the oil comes from the outside part of the whale. Just under the whale's skin there is a thick layer of fat called blubber. This blubber is as much as fifteen inches thick. When it is boiled and melted, the oil comes out and is collected and stored in barrels in the bottom of the ship. When the ship returns home, the owners of the ship sell the oil. There might be as much as fifty barrels of oil taken from just one whale. But it takes a huge amount of work to get a fish that weighs ninety tons into fifty barrels!

One end of a rope was tied to the ship and the other end to a man. The man was lowered onto the whale and began cutting strips of blubber from its body. It was almost like peeling the skin from an orange. After a strip was cut loose, a huge hook (itself weighing as much as a hundred pounds) was used to lift the blubber to the deck of the ship. There, the strips were cut into smaller pieces that would fit into the boiling pots. Up and down went the hook. The men pulling the ropes were completely tired out by the time the work was done. It had taken the whole morning.

The one last job was to remove the head of the whale. Deep inside the Sperm whale's head is the valuable stuff known as spermaceti, used to make expensive perfumes. The Sperm whale's head is about twenty-five feet long. You can imagine how heavy it must be! It would have tipped our boat over had we tried to lift it over the side of the ship, as we had lifted the pieces of blubber.

Instead, once it had been cut from the rest of the body, the head was pulled just out of the water and hung to the outside of the ship. Later, the spermaceti could be dug from its very center.

When all the work was done, Ahab shouted out, "Haul in the chains! Cut the rest of the whale loose from the ship!"

The peeled skeleton was released and began to float into the distance. Shrieking sea birds swooped down and tore away scraps of skin. Sharks swarmed around, as they fought for one last vicious bite at what was left of this proud beast.

It was noon, and the crew went below for their dinner. The deck was quiet, and the sea was calm. Captain Ahab came out of his cabin. After he had taken a short walk around the deck, he stopped to stare over the side at the whale's head. He looked intently into its dead eyes.

"Speak, ye giant, mysterious head. Speak, and tell me the secrets you hide about the seas. Tell me everything ye know. But now I see ye cannot talk. Ye hold the secrets to which I long to know the answers, but ye cannot speak a single word. Ye cannot tell me what I need to know."

Ahab's strange talk was ended by a cry from the mast above. "Sail ho!" cried the voice. "Sail ho! A ship ahead!"

"Aye? Well, now, that's cheerful news. If this dead whale will tell me nothing, perhaps there's news of Moby Dick on this ship."

As soon as the other ship came near, Ahab cried, "Have ye seen the White Whale?"

CHAPTER FIFTEEN

The Jeroboam

Captain Mayhew of the *Jeroboam* gave us some bad news. It seemed that not long after the crew of the *Jeroboam* had left home, they met a ship that warned them of the dangers of hunting Moby Dick. In spite of this, a year or two later, upon sighting Moby Dick, Captain Mayhew's chief mate, Macey, burned with desire to attack him.

Mayhew, ignoring the warnings, agreed to let Macey lower a boat. Macey talked five other men into going with him, and after a hard chase they were able to get one harpoon into the whale. But then the monstrous white hump rose from beneath Macey's boat. As the horrified crew

watched from the ship, poor Macey was tossed fifty yards into the air and he disappeared into the sea, never to be seen again.

When he had finished his story, Mayhew asked Ahab if he still was going to hunt Moby Dick. To this Ahab answered, "Aye. I will hunt him around the world!"

"Think, think of Macey down there at the bottom of the ocean!" said Mayhew. "Think of that man who attacked Moby Dick. Beware, or you will come to the same end. You, too, will be dead and lost to the sea."

Ahab sneered, with no comment on this frightening tale. Instead, he went on to tell Mayhew that he had a letter for the *Jeroboam*. It had been given to him to deliver in case they should meet. Starbuck went below deck to get the letter, returned, and handed it to Ahab.

"Well, look here," Ahab said. "The letter is for that poor Macey. And he's dead. Ah, well. I'll give it to you just the same."

"Nay! Keep the letter. You'll soon be going the same way as Macey. You can deliver it to him yourself!"

"Curse ye, ye mad fool!" screamed Ahab.

The two ships parted, and the sails of the *Jeroboam* became a faint speck in the distance.

I shuddered at what I had heard. The stories about the White Whale were true. Moby Dick was a killer!

CHAPTER SIXTEEN

Stubb and Flask Kill a Right Whale

Not many days after meeting the *Jeroboam*, a school of Right whales was sighted. The Right whale is not as valuable as the Sperm whale, but Ahab told Stubb and Flask to attack. Within a short time, both crews had harpoons in one of the whales.

I watched from the deck as the whale swam in circles around the ship, towing the two boats behind him. After some deep dives and a fierce fight, the whale gave up and lay floating near the ship. Hundreds of sharks soon began to circle, but before they could do much damage we had the whale alongside.

When the blubber had been stripped and loaded, the Right whale's head was removed and hung on the ship's side opposite from the head of the Sperm whale still hanging there.

As the crew continued working, Stubb and Flask stood looking at the Right whale's head. I heard Stubb tell Flask that the only reason we had bothered to kill such a whale was to make Fedallah happy. Stubb said he had heard Fedallah whispering to Ahab. The next thing he knew, Ahab had agreed to kill the Right whale and hang its head on the ship for good luck.

Stubb had never heard of such a thing in all his years at sea. He told Flask that this strange Fedallah would bring no good luck at all. Stubb thought Fedallah was a devil who had Ahab under his control.

I wished I had not heard the two mates. I was a happy man when I left home. I had been ready to face the dangers of the sea and the risks in hunting great whales. I had never thought I would have a crazy captain who took advice from some evil, devilish harpooner.

I turned away from Stubb and Flask and saw Fedallah staring at the whales' heads. Just in front of Fedallah stood Ahab so that Fedallah was in his shadow. Wherever Ahab moved, his shadow took Fedallah with it.

Day turned to dusk, and dusk turned to night. Our ship sailed on, balanced on either side by whale heads. I wished that Ahab's mind were more balanced.

CHAPTER SEVENTEEN

A Milky Bath

The next morning, with no whales in sight to hunt, it came time to dig into the mammoth head of the Sperm whale and pull out the valuable spermaceti.

The head of the Sperm whale has two parts. The huge mouth and jaw make up the lower half. The upper half is a shell of bone and muscle. Inside that shell is what is called the whale's case. It is like one huge barrel. In a large whale, such as the one we had killed, there could be as much as five hundred gallons of spermaceti.

Once the jaw was cut loose, the harpooners became dentists. Queequeg, Daggoo, and Tashtego

carefully pulled each and every ivory tooth. There are usually forty-two in all. The rest of the jaw was cut into pieces of bone and stored below. The bone and teeth would be made into beautiful carvings and sold in shops all over the world. Now that the dental work was done, it was time to get at the top part of the head still hanging from the ship.

Nimble as a cat, Tashtego climbed up the mast and out onto one of the cross arms until he was directly above the whale's head. Then he lowered himself hand-over-hand down a rope that he had looped over the cross arm. When he was standing on that slippery, rocking head, he asked for his sharp cutting spear and began to search for the exact spot to begin breaking into the head. As carefully as a treasure hunter, he cut a hole in the head.

A bucket with a line attached to it was lowered to him. The other end of the line was held tightly by men on the deck above. Tashtego dropped the bucket down through the hole he had cut in the head. When he raised it, it was full of a bubbling, milky liquid. The bucket was pulled up to the deck, emptied in a large tub, and sent back down to Tashtego. On and on the work went. Several tubs had been filled with the sweet-smelling liquid, and the hole in the whale's head was now over twenty feet deep. Then a strange accident happened.

Whether it was that wild Indian's carelessness or the slippery, oozy surface on which Tashtego stood, we never knew—but all of a sudden, poor Tashtego fell head-first into the hole. With a horrible, oily gurgling, he went out of sight!

"Man overboard!" cried Daggoo. "Swing the bucket over to me!" Putting one foot into the bucket, and holding the line with his hands to steady himself, he shouted at us to lower him to the top of the whale's head. Still hanging just above the whale, he rammed the bucket down into the hole in the whale's head, hoping Tashtego might grab it.

"In heaven's name, man," cried Stubb, "are you trying to kill the man? How will that help him, jamming that iron bucket on top of his head? Avast! Back off! Stop!"

At that instant, the hooks holding the head to the boat tore loose. With a thunderous boom, the giant head crashed into the sea. This left poor

Daggoo hanging to the lines in mid-air. Tashtego, now buried alive, was sinking to the bottom of the sea. Suddenly, Queequeg rushed to the side of the ship. My brave friend dived to the rescue. Every eye onboard was watching the water below, looking for some ripple or sign of the two harpooners. Several of the crew scrambled into a boat and lowered it to the water.

"Ha! Ha!" cried Daggoo. We saw an arm pop up from the blue waters like an arm pushing up through the grass above a grave.

"Both! Both! It's both of them!" yelled Daggoo with a joyful shout. Queequeg appeared, swimming with one hand and holding Tashtego's long hair with the other. Both men were pulled into the waiting boat and quickly brought up to the deck. It took some time before Tashtego opened his eyes. Queequeg lay beside his friend, too tired to move.

I fell asleep that evening thinking of Queequeg's courage and the goodness that must be in his heart. Captain Ahab had not done a thing to help save Tashtego. Instead, it was the tall savage from the islands of the Pacific whose mercy and daring gave new life to this Indian from Massachusetts. I decided there were good men all around this great world, men who could care about each other.

CHAPTER EIGHTEEN

The Grand Army

With a fair, fresh wind, the *Pequod* sailed on. We approached the strait of Sundra which passes between the islands of Sumatra and Java. Here we would leave the Indian Ocean and enter the China Seas. This was the gateway to the riches and mysteries of an oriental world, full of spices, silks, jewels, gold, and ivory.

It was Ahab's plan to go from here, past the Philippine Islands, and into the seas of Japan. On this course, we would pass through waters known to have great numbers of Sperm whales. It was also the route that Ahab thought would take us to seas where Moby Dick had most often been seen.

Sometimes in this area, Sperm whales get together in herds—as if the whales have had *enough* of being chased through four oceans and decide to join up in one big army. Some old sailors said that it sometimes looked as though there were a thousand or more spouts at one time. So the lookouts were ordered to keep a sharp eye. The soft, green palm trees waved and bowed to us from the island off our right side, and the crisp smell of cinnamon filled the air. It was a peaceful paradise. Shouts from the lookouts ended the quiet peace.

Straight ahead of our ship a great army of whales was shooting more sparkling spouts into the air than most men would see in their whole lives. They were the tall, single bursts of Sperm whales. The sea looked like a whole city of cheerful chimneys on a cold morning.

We increased our speed and started the chase. The harpooners and the rest of the crews were scrambling to their boats. Loud cheers went up. It looked as though we had a chance to capture several whales. Maybe Moby Dick himself would be among them!

Just when our luck seemed to be getting better, Tashtego suddenly began shouting and pointing to something behind us.

Ahab spun around on his ivory leg and spotted an army of a different kind. "Malay savages behind us!" he cried. "Faster ahead! Outrun them!"

Coming at us from behind were boats full of bloodthirsty island natives. Ahab began pacing back and forth. Looking forward he saw the monsters he chased, and looking back he saw the pirates chasing him. Thoughts of a white devil

ahead of him and the dark devils behind him were more than his mind could stand. A black look came into his eyes, and the white leg tapped more quickly.

In the end we were lucky. A wind came up that increased our speed and left the pirates falling behind. We turned our eyes to the whales ahead. We were pulling nearer to them, and orders were given to lower the boats. As soon as the boats were in the water, the whales, as if they knew we were after them, began increasing their speed.

Stripped to our undershirts, we pulled the oars until it felt as though our arms would drop off. After several hours of back-breaking rowing, the whales slowed down and began to break into smaller groups. They were swimming in slow circles directly in front of us. Queequeg was the first to send his harpoon flying into one of the whales.

The instant Queequeg's harpoon was in him, the whale began thrashing and turning. His spout threw a burst of spray in our faces. His great tail, which I could see was nearly twenty feet wide, churned the water around us. Soon we were being pulled along behind the whale, right through the whole herd of whales that was around us on every side. The harpoon lines became knotted and snarled together in the bottom of the boat. As the whales rolled and slid over one another trying to break free, the lines began to wrap around their bodies. Before long, we saw that the only way out of the mess we were in was to cut the lines and release the whales.

As it turned out, after all the hard work and danger, our three boats captured just one whale in all. Flask had killed a whale early in the chase. Otherwise, we would have come away empty-handed.

There is an old saying in this business—the more whales, the less fish. I knew then what that meant—the more whales, the fewer you catch.

CHAPTER NINETEEN

A Warning Not Taken

"Ship, ahoy! Have ye seen the White Whale?" Ahab's familiar cry rang out, as a ship with an English flag sailed toward our ship. It was the *Samuel Enderby* of London.

The old man stood at the ship's side, his ivory leg in plain sight. As the ships drew nearer to each other, we saw that one arm of the English captain's jacket was empty and hung loosely at his side.

"Have ye seen the White Whale?" Ahab cried a second time.

"Do you see this?" answered the stranger, pulling an arm of white Sperm whale bone from under his jacket and waving it above his head.

"Man my boat!" screamed Ahab. "Prepare to lower!"

In less than a minute he was in his boat sitting below the English ship. "Tell me, man. Tell me quick! Where did ye see the White Whale?"

"There I saw him! There on the Equator last year," said the captain, his dead, white arm pointing toward the East.

"And he took your arm from you, did he?" asked Ahab.

"He did. And did he take your leg?"

"Tell me the story. Tell me the story!" Ahab shouted, becoming more excited.

The Englishman said that he had been hunting in the area of the Equator for the first time and, until then, had never heard of Moby Dick. One day, after he had found a small herd of whales and gotten a harpoon into one of them, a giant white whale rose from the deep and began snapping at the line as if he were trying to free the other whale.

"And his hump!—was it huge and wrinkled, and did it have a harpoon stuck in it?" asked Ahab.

"That it did," the captain went on. "And

when I put my own harpoon in him, he dragged me from my boat. The line hooked around my arm and tore it from my shoulder."

"That's him! That's Moby Dick!" shouted Ahab. "I put that first harpoon in him just before he took my leg. Have ye seen him since?"

"Twice more I've seen him, but I didn't chase him. I don't need to give up my other arm. I know when I've met my match. There are other whales in the sea."

"Which way did he go? Where will I find him?" Ahab cried.

"You better leave him alone," warned the Englishman, waving his whale-bone arm.

"I cannot leave him alone. I must hunt him," said Ahab. "He draws me to him. Tell me, man, what direction did he go?"

"Good heavens! What's the matter with you?" said the other captain. "He was heading east, I think." Then he turned, whispering to Fedallah, "Is your captain crazy?"

Putting his finger to his lips as if to silence the Englishman, Fedallah hurried Ahab back into his boat. Ahab's phantom, eerie crew wasted no time rowing Ahab back toward the *Pequod*.

The Englishman shouted for Ahab to listen to him, but Ahab stared straight ahead through cold, dark eyes that shone like black marbles. The wild look on Ahab's face as he struggled back up to the *Pequod*'s deck sent cold chills through me. I had a feeling that things were going to get worse, but I had no idea how *much* worse.

CHAPTER TWENTY

A New White Leg

As soon as he set foot and stump on deck, Ahab began the most furious pacing back and forth. Then, as if he wanted to look everywhere at the same time, he stuck his ivory leg in the hole in the deck and began spinning around and around in circles like a top. Suddenly, there was a sharp, screeching snap as the ivory leg broke in two. With a hateful look, Ahab ordered the carpenter and blacksmith to make him another leg.

The men worked straight through the night until a new leg was finished and fastened to Ahab's knee. Without a word of thanks, Ahab whirled and rushed back to the deck where he stood for the whole day and night. His eyes never left the seas in front of him.

There would not be much rest from now on. We were getting closer to Moby Dick.

The next day we had another kind of problem.

CHAPTER TWENTY-ONE

Queequeg's Coffin

Once a whale ship has begun to fill its barrels with oil, the men pour water over the barrels every few days to keep them damp. The dampness tightens the wood and keeps the valuable treasure from leaking out. After the barrels have been soaked, the water is pumped out and the seamen look closely at this water. If there is any sign of whale oil in the water, it means there is a leak. As you can imagine, after risking their lives to collect the oil, this causes great concern among the crew.

The pumping had been done according to schedule, and a leak was found. The bad news was passed to Starbuck, and he went to Ahab's cabin to report the serious problem. Starbuck found Ahab bent over his desk making marks on maps where Moby Dick had been seen.

"The oil is leaking down in the hold of the ship, sir. We must drop sails, pull up the barrels, and repair the leak."

"What's that ye say?" shouted Ahab. "Curse ye, man. We'll not stop for a second, not when we're nearing Moby Dick. Stop to fix some stupid barrels? Full ahead, I say!" cried Ahab, pointing to the charts in front of him.

"If we don't fix the leak, sir, we'll lose in one day all the precious oil we've come twenty thousand miles to get."

"Let it leak! I am in control of this ship, and I say let the blasted oil leak!"

Starbuck's face reddened. He begged Ahab to listen to him. This threw Ahab into a rage. He grabbed a gun from the wall, and pointed it at Starbuck.

Starbuck slowly straightened and looked into Ahab's eyes. "Thou hast angered me, sir. But thou hast no reason to fear me. I will tell thee whom thou must fear, Captain Ahab. Let Ahab beware

of Ahab! Beware of thyself, old man."

Starbuck turned and left, leaving Ahab alone. Soon after, his order to drop all sails and repair the barrels rang out across the decks.

The crew sprang into action and began the difficult, messy work of digging through the slimy, cold waters in the very bottom of the ship. Each barrel was moved until the leaks were found and fixed. Queequeg worked harder than I've ever seen a man work, slithering around the barrels like a spotted lizard at the bottom of a well. Sadly, with all the sweating down in that dampness, Queequeg became chilled, and for a few days became so sick that I was afraid he might die.

We put Queequeg into bed and wrapped him up to keep him warm. There he lay, poor fellow, his color becoming gray and his eyes becoming more hollow as the days wore on. Not one man in the crew gave up on him, though. Then, all at once, Queequeg's eyelids fluttered, and his faint voice made a strange request.

Taking the hand of the sailor nearest to him, Queequeg whispered that he remembered the whalers of Nantucket always being laid in little wooden canoes when they died. Since this was also what the people of his native island did, Queequeg wondered if we could build a small canoe that would be his coffin. I can tell you, there was nothing we would not do for this brave man. The carpenter soon had built a canoe of the finest wood he could find.

When the canoe was brought to him, Queequeg asked that we put him in it and that his harpoon be placed at his side. Then he asked us to bring him his little wooden god, Yojo, and his boat paddle. When all of this had been done, Queequeg closed his eyes and spoke not a word for a long time.

When his eyes finally opened, there was a new shine in them, and the happy crew knew that he was getting well. A few days later, when Queequeg's strength had returned, he found a board in the carpenter's shop and began making a cover for the canoe-coffin. He spent hours carving native figures and designs on the cover, which looked like the tattoos on his body. Queequeg then said that he was ready to go back to hunting whales. He stored his harpoon and clothing in the coffin and joined the rest of the crew on deck.

CHAPTER TWENTY-TWO

The Devil's Harpoon

Our sails filled by a friendly breeze, we left the islands behind us and glided at last into the great Pacific. Oh, how I had dreamed of these seas, this most watery part of the world. This was the very place I had pictured in my mind as I packed my suitcase many months and thousands of miles ago—the Pacific, the sea of peace. But sometimes, peaceful dreams can become nightmares.

The Pacific brought no peace to Ahab. To him, the Pacific meant only that he was getting nearer to the hated White Whale. The fires of revenge burned hotter in his soul, and he left his watch on deck only to sleep. But we even heard him cry out in his sleep, "She blows! The White Whale blows! She spouts thick blood!" The madness in the things he did grew worse.

One morning, Ahab ordered that the blacksmith build a harpoon of the hardest steel. When its point had been made sharp, he called Queequeg, Tashtego and Daggoo to his cabin. Taking blood from each of their arms, he dipped the tip of the harpoon into it and baptized the harpoon in the name of the devil. "This will be the harpoon that kills Moby Dick," he shrieked. As the days went on, the harpoon never left his hand as he thumped and tapped back and forth on his dead, white leg.

When Queequeg told me what had happened during that evil baptism, my dreams of peace ended—my nightmare had begun.

CHAPTER TWENTY-THREE

The Happy Bachelor

As we sailed farther into the heart of the Japanese whaling grounds, we began to see whales all around us. Often, in mild, pleasant weather, we spent ten or twenty hours each day pulling oars as we chased after them, but we had no luck. On one of these calm days, a ship came into sight. She was a ship from Nantucket named the *Bachelor*.

As the ship came closer, we saw she was on her way home, every barrel full of rich oil. Colorful flags flew from her masts, and the crew was dancing and singing. Every member of the crew wore a smile on his face. The happy captain stood up. Ahab also stood on his deck, shaggy, dark, and full of gloom.

"Come aboard, come aboard!" cried the laughing captain of the merry ship.

"Have ye seen the White Whale?" Ahab replied, scowling.

"No, only heard of him. But I don't believe in him at all. Come aboard!"

"Ye are too jolly! Sail on," muttered Ahab.

"Nonsense! Come aboard and join our party. We'll take that black look from your face," answered the captain of the *Bachelor*.

"I have no interest in your happy party," said Ahab. "Ye are a full ship. We are an empty ship. So, go your way, and I will go mine."

The two ships passed. The laughter of the *Bachelor* died away in the distance. Ahab stared at the ship until it was gone. Then he reached into his pocket and pulled out a small bottle. In the bottle were a few grains of sand from America. After looking for several minutes at the small reminder of home, he spun around on his ivory leg and ordered the crew to sail at full speed on a course that would lead him to Moby Dick.

CHAPTER TWENTY-FOUR

Fedallah's Dark Riddle

We were not a happy crew after our meeting with the *Bachelor*. The joy and laughter of the men heading for home showed us how dark and unhappy things were on the *Pequod*. We needed something to cheer us up. The following day brought a little good luck that took our minds off our problems, at least for awhile.

Just before noon, whales were found and four were killed—one by Ahab. It was late in the afternoon when the chase ended, and by the time we had three of the four whales tied to the ship, the sun was setting. The crews were in a good mood.

The whale Ahab's crew had killed had not yet been brought to the ship. As darkness came, Ahab ordered his crew to stay in the boat next to their whale. There Ahab sat, bobbing up and down on the waves, staring at the whale. He could not get his hatred and bitterness toward Moby Dick out of his mind. With these dark thoughts circling in his mind, Ahab fell asleep.

Fedallah was now the only one awake in Ahab's boat. He sat quietly, mysteriously, watching the sharks twist and turn around the dead whale. One of them flapped against the side of the boat. Ahab woke up and saw Fedallah's shadowy face.

"I have had a dream, Fedallah," Ahab said. "I have dreamed of a hearse coming to carry my body away."

"Didn't I tell you of that dark mystery, old man?" said Fedallah. "You will have neither a hearse nor a coffin. But you will see two hearses on the sea before you die. The first will be one not made by human hands. The second hearse will be made only of wood grown in America."

Ahab laughed and refused to believe Fedallah.

"Believe it or not, old man. You cannot die

until these things happen. And hear these words. I shall go before you to lead the way. Even after I have gone ahead of you to death, you will see me again."

"What? Ye shall pilot me and lead me to my death?" said Ahab. "Well, let me tell ye something. Your foolish predictions only make me believe that I *shall* kill Moby Dick and still live."

"Listen closely, Ahab," warned Fedallah. "A rope will kill you."

"Never!" said Ahab. "Your warnings are so impossible to believe that I don't think I shall ever die." Ahab laughed and turned away.

Nothing more was said. The gray dawn came on, and the sleeping crew awoke. Before noon, the dead whale was brought to the ship.

CHAPTER TWENTY-FIVE

The Candles

In a few days' time, we turned toward the Equator where Moby Dick had been seen. Several of the men began looking at the gold doubloon nailed to the mast, wondering who would get the prize. The ship was full of excitement. The excitement turned to terror that evening when we ran into a typhoon, the worst kind of storm there is.

The storm raged and grew worse as the night grew darker. Our sails were ripped from their masts. Sky and sea roared. The night skies were split with thunder and blazed with the lightning. Starbuck stood hanging to a line and wondered if it could get any worse. It did. Everything was out of our control. In the middle of all this fury, we saw Ahab making his way toward the ship's bare mast and pointing to the sky with his cursed harpoon.

Looking up, we saw the tops of the three masts suddenly throw off sparks and burst into flame. They looked like three gigantic candles burning before an altar. It was as if God's burning finger had been laid upon the ship.

"Have mercy on us all!" cried Stubb.

"Aye, aye, men!" shouted Ahab. "Look up at it. It is a sign. The white flame lights the way to the White Whale! The lightning is a light that leaps out of darkness, but I am a darkness that leaps out of light!"

When he spoke those words, Ahab's harpoon burst into fire and burned like a snake's tongue. Starbuck grabbed Ahab's arm. "God is against thee, old man. Beware! It is a bad journey. Let me turn the ship around and head home while we can."

The crew became restless and moved to follow Starbuck's advice. Ahab snatched the burning harpoon and held it up to the crew, swearing that he would use it on them if they

moved a muscle to turn the ship around.

"I have sworn to kill the White Whale, and ye are sworn to follow me! There is no turning back." Holding the harpoon to his lips, he blew out the flame and screamed, "I blow out the last fear!"

The sailors turned from him in terror. Only Starbuck stayed to try to talk to Ahab. But it was no use. Ahab ordered him to hold course and sail through the typhoon against the powerful forces of nature.

CHAPTER TWENTY-SIX

The Life Buoy

Steering south-eastward now, we moved even closer to the Equator and found ourselves in calm waters. The calm was suddenly broken by cries from the water. The sailor keeping the first watch of the morning had fallen from his post and was struggling for dear life to keep his head above water. An empty barrel was thrown as a life buoy, but it had become cracked and sank to the bottom along with the poor young sailor.

Queequeg suggested that since we now had no life preserver for future emergencies, we should make one from his own canoe-coffin. Starbuck ordered the coffin brought up from below, and the carpenter nailed the cover shut and sealed the cracks with tar so it would float. When they were finished, we hung it on the back of our ship.

Ahab laughed and made fun of the idea of using a box made for death as something that might save a life. Queequeg, bless him, seemed to know what he was doing. I found out later just how wise an idea this was. You shall find out, too.

CHAPTER TWENTY-SEVEN

Sad Rachel

The next day, still sad about the loss of our young sailor, we met the *Rachel*, a ship full of a sadness of much the same kind.

As the ship pulled near, we could see that her crew seemed gloomy. Her captain stood to speak, but before he could get a word out, Ahab's voice rang out.

"Have ye seen the White Whale?"

"Aye, yesterday. Have you seen a lost whaleboat anywhere?"

Ahab could hardly control his joy when he heard that Moby Dick might be near. But before he could speak, the other captain had lowered a boat and climbed aboard our ship. He now faced Ahab, his eyes full of pain and worry. Ahab saw that he was a man from Nantucket whom he knew, but made no effort to greet him.

It seemed that the afternoon before, the *Rachel* had sighted Moby Dick's white hump and sent four boats after him. One boat had gotten a harpoon in him, but the whale had dived below and never came back up. The captain had called in his boats when it became dark. Only three had come back. The fourth, along with its crew, was missing. The *Rachel* had searched all night with no luck.

Having told his sad story, the captain asked Ahab to join with him in the search for his crew. Ahab gave him a cold look and made no offer to help.

"My boy—my own son—is among that crew! For God's sake, I beg you! Just help me for forty-eight hours. I'll gladly pay you. He's but a little lad, only twelve years old." The captain's eyes filled with tears.

Still, Ahab stood like a stone, his eyes cold and empty.

"I know you have a son of your own, Captain

Ahab. Think of him, safe and warm back home. Do for me what you would have me do for you." Then the captain added, "I will not go until you've agreed to help me."

"Away with ye!" cried Ahab. "Captain Gardiner, I will not do it. Even now, I am losing time. Good-bye. Good-bye. God bless ye, man, and may I forgive myself, but I must go. Starbuck, in three minutes get all the strangers off the ship and make her ready to sail!" Ahab turned and went into his cabin.

Gardiner, without a word, hurried down the side of the ship and back to his own. My heart ached as I watched his ship sail back and forth, stopping to search every dark spot in the sea.

She was like Rachel in the Bible, weeping for her children because they were not yet found.

CHAPTER TWENTY-EIGHT

We Meet the Delight

A ship with the name *Delight* had been sighted. I hoped that this was a good sign, for we all needed something to delight us right now. My hopes soon were destroyed by the news the ship brought. As the *Delight* came nearer, we saw a smashed whaleboat hanging from her side.

"Have ye seen the White Whale?" shouted Ahab.

"Look!" said the hollow-cheeked captain, pointing to the wrecked boat.

"Have ye killed him?" Ahab asked.

"The harpoon has not been made that will ever do that. I am burying the first of five men he killed."

"Not made?" cried Ahab, holding his harpoon

above his head. "I hold in my hand his death, baptized in blood and hardened by lightning bolts."

"Then God be with you, old man." The captain turned to his crew and ordered that they prepare to release the body of the dead sailor to its ocean grave. He began to pray.

"Sail on! Sail on!" screamed Ahab. But we had not sailed quickly enough to avoid hearing the splash of the body as it fell into the sea.

We turned away from the *Delight*. Her captain saw the coffin hanging on the rear of our ship. "Ha! Look men!" he cried. "She turns her back on our sad burial and shows us her own coffin!"

As we headed east under full sail, my fears returned. The *Delight* had brought no delight.

CHAPTER TWENTY-NINE

The Chase — First Day

From that moment on, Ahab would not leave the deck. With weird Fedallah at his side, he paced, and turned, and whirled from one end of the ship to the other. What little he ate, he ate standing up.

One night, Ahab stopped short in the middle of his pacing. He raised his face to the sky and began sniffing the air like a hunting dog. He said he could smell a whale and ordered the men to drop the sails and stay in that spot for the night. His nose proved right, for at daybreak a faint rippling path in the sea told us that something below was stirring the surface.

"Man the mastheads! Call all hands! Tell me what ye see!"

When the crew reported they saw nothing, Ahab ordered that he be lifted to the top of the mast. When he was nearly at the top, he let out a wild shriek. "There she blows! There she blows! A hump like a huge hill of snow! It is Moby Dick!"

The crew rushed to the ship's side to get a look at the thing they had been chasing for over two years. There, about a mile ahead, the whale rolled his hump and sent his spout into the air. The silent, silvery jet reminded the crew of the mysterious spirit spout they had seen in the moonlight of other oceans.

"And did none of ye see it?" asked Ahab. "Was I the first? Yes, it was I. The gold doubloon is mine. None of ye could have found the White Whale. Only I! There he is again! Again! He dives! Drop sails! Stand by to lower three boats. Starbuck, ye stay here and take care of the ship. Lower me from the mast! Faster! Now boats! To the boats!"

Soon all the boats but Starbuck's were dropped. Ahab's crew took the lead boat. The oars pulled through the water as all three crews

began to make their way out. Fedallah stood in Ahab's boat; a pale death-glimmer lit up his sunken eyes. Like silent fish, the boats sailed through the sea toward the White Whale.

The ocean became calm and smooth as if a carpet had been thrown over its waves. Ahab could see the huge wrinkled hump now as it rose in front of him. Hundreds of white sea birds circled above his boat. Now and then one swooped down to land on a harpoon that stuck straight up from the white back of the whale. Moby Dick moved on quietly, still hiding his lower body below the surface.

Suddenly, the calm was broken and the water exploded as the beast arched its body into the air, its cruel jaws wide open. Just as suddenly it dove, throwing its monstrous tail twenty feet above the sea before it went out of sight. The white birds still circled above the pool where the whale had last been seen.

With their oars in the air, the three boats floated quietly and waited for Moby Dick. Ahab stared into the water—looking, watching, waiting. Ahab's eyes were on a white spot rising upward from below and growing larger every second that it rose. In the next instant, Moby Dick's huge jaw with its two rows of crooked teeth burst through the surface. Ahab grabbed his special harpoon and rushed to the front of his boat. As if he knew Ahab's plan, the whale rolled

on its side, opened its jaws, fastened them around Ahab's boat, and began shaking it like a cat playing with a mouse. Furious with the creature he hated and seeing it so near to him, Ahab grabbed the jawbone with his bare hands and wildly tried to pull it free of its grip on his boat. The bone slipped from his hands. But then the huge jaws closed just six inches from Ahab's head like a pair of huge scissors. Ahab's boat snapped in two like a toothpick. Ahab was tossed into the sea like a rag doll.

Moby Dick backed away and watched from a distance for a moment. The crew floated helplessly in the two halves of the boat. All at once, the whale began swimming in circles round and round the boat. Moby Dick swam faster and faster, as if the sight of the splintered boat angered him. Ahab's head popped in and out of the bubbling foam. He shouted for Starbuck to steer the ship at the whale. As the *Pequod* came at him, Moby Dick swam away. The boats rushed to pick up their captain. Ahab tumbled into Stubb's boat. His eyes were bloodshot, and his hair was twisted and caked with salt.

"The harpoon," he gasped. "Is it safe?"

"Aye, sir, for it was never thrown. It is here with me," answered Stubb.

When Ahab was back aboard the ship, Starbuck tried again to talk him into giving up the madness. But the demons within Ahab would not let him go.

A light fog crept over the water. A few hundred yards from the ship, a mountainous forehead broke the water's surface and waited. The first day had been a good one for Moby Dick.

CHAPTER THIRTY

The Chase — Second Day

Our ship had stayed on the same course all night. Ahab knew that whales usually continued in the same direction. So, when he came on deck the next morning, he was sure Moby Dick could not be far away.

"Have ye seen him?" shouted Ahab to the lookouts on the masts.

"Nothing yet, sir. Not a thing," came the reply.

"All men on deck! Faster ahead at full sail on our same course! He swims faster than I thought, but he'll not escape. I've come around the world to kill him, and kill him I will." Ahab barked out his orders in rapid bursts.

"There she blows! There blows a spout straight ahead!" came a cry from the mast.

"Aye, ha, ha!" said Stubb. "I knew it. I knew you'd not escape, whale. A madman is after you. Ahab will drain you of your blood!"

Thirty men sprang into action, and all eyes searched the sea. For a long time they saw nothing. Suddenly, shouts rang out as Moby Dick's whole body burst forth not a mile in front of the ship.

"There she leaps! She breaches!" was the cry, as the whale came completely out of the water before crashing back to the surface.

"Yes! Lift yourself one last time to the sun, Moby Dick!" cried Ahab. "Your harpoon and your hour of death are near! Stand by all boats!"

Three boats were lowered to the water. As he had the previous day, Ahab told Starbuck to stay on the ship and keep close to the boats. Ahab and his crew leaped into one of the three boats, Fedallah standing at the front.

As if he had decided on a quick strike of his own, Moby Dick had turned and now was headed directly at the boats. Ahab shouted for the crews to stay where they were and meet the whale head-on.

The whale's furious speed and lashing tail tossed the boats like toy ships in a child's bathtub. Harpoons were thrown and stuck in his back. Moby Dick only swam faster and made charge after charge. The lines attached to the harpoons became tangled and wrapped around all three boats. Ahab cut the lines from his harpoon, but Moby Dick dragged the other two boats behind him, and with one flip of his tail threw the boats into the air and the men into the sea.

Stubb and Flask screamed out for help as they fought to stay afloat. Sharks began to circle. Ahab, free of the lines, turned his boat toward them. At that instant, Moby Dick came up from the depths at full speed and crashed his head into the bottom of Ahab's boat. The boat rose straight up in the air as if it had been shot from a cannon. It tumbled over and over and fell back to the sea, its crew trapped beneath. Ahab made his way out from under the crushed boat and clung to its splintered side. As if satisfied, Moby Dick backed away and watched quietly for a moment. Then he turned his broad tail and swam slowly away.

When the fury of the battle had ended, Starbuck brought the ship into position to rescue

the men. One by one, the men and pieces of the boats were pulled from the water. As Ahab was brought up we saw that his ivory leg had been snapped off, leaving but a short, sharp splinter. He leaned on Starbuck's shoulder and ordered that the spare boats be made ready. The carpenter promised to make him a new leg.

After asking about Moby Dick and the direction he had headed, Ahab ordered a roll call of the crew to see if any were missing. There was no sign of Fedallah. Starbuck told Ahab he had seen the lines of the harpoon wrap around Fedallah. He was sure that Moby Dick had dragged Fedallah under. Ahab whispered something under his breath:

"Fedallah—Fedallah!—gone, gone? *And he told me he would die before me!* Yet he also said *I would see him again before I die.* What's that to mean? It's a tough riddle, but I'll solve it."

As with the evening before, we dropped sail and got ready for a third battle. The sounds of hammers, saws, and grindstones were heard all night as the crews prepared spare boats and sharpened new harpoons. Meanwhile, the carpenter built a new leg for Ahab out of a piece of Ahab's own wrecked boat. Those who had not been injured stayed busy making bandages for the others' wounds.

Ahab swore that tomorrow would be the last day of Moby Dick's life. He remained on deck a long while, staring into the distance. His eyes never left the sea as shadows cast by the full moon flickered back and forth across the ugly scar on his face. In the distance, another scarred head waited, as before.

CHAPTER THIRTY-ONE

The Chase — Third Day

The morning of the third day dawned fair and fresh. The sea was quiet and calm—almost too calm. Just as soon as the sun had risen, every mast was dotted with men on daylight watch.

"D'ye see him?" cried Ahab. But the whale was nowhere in sight.

"Just keep following that path of ripples his great tail leaves for us. Hold a straight course. What a lovely day again! It seems a new world— a summer house to the angels. A nicer day could not dawn upon this world. The warm winds blow my good ship on, and something as steady as the wind blows my soul along. On with it! Aloft there, in the masts! What d'ye see?"

"Nothing, sir."

"Nothing! Do none of ye see the White Whale? And it's nearly noon! Yes, the sun, I see it now. It must be that we sailed past him in the night. Aye, he's chasing *me* now, and I am not chasing *him*. That's bad. Turn around! Sail back the way we came!"

Returning in the opposite direction, the *Pequod* sailed directly against the wind, plowing through the foam of its own path.

"Now he steers against the wind for the open jaw," murmured Starbuck. "God keep us, but already my bones feel damp and my flesh wet from the inside. I fear that I disobey my God by obeying him!"

"Swing me up to the mast!" screamed Ahab. "We should meet him soon."

A whole hour passed. Even the air around us seemed to hold its breath. But at last, Ahab spied the spout again.

"Forehead to forehead I meet thee, this third time, Moby Dick! He's too far off to lower boats yet, Mr. Starbuck. He travels fast and I must get down from here. But let me have one last look at

the sea from here—an old sight, but somehow still so young. It hasn't changed a bit since I first saw it as a boy from the sand hills of Nantucket. It's the same—the same to Noah as to me.

"But good-bye, farewell, old ship. We both grow old together. And what about Fedallah? He said I would see him again before I die. But where? Will I have eyes at the bottom of the sea if I should happen to go down those dark stairs? Good-bye, masthead. Keep a good eye upon the whale while I'm gone. We'll talk tomorrow—no, tonight, when Moby Dick is dead."

Ahab gave the word and was steadily lowered through the blue air to the deck. Shortly, the boats were lowered. Ahab waved from his boat to Starbuck on deck.

"Starbuck!"

"Sir?"

"For the third time my soul sets out on this hunt, Starbuck."

"Aye, sir. That is as thou would have it."

"Some ships sail from home and are never seen again, Starbuck."

"It's true, sir—sad, but true."

"Starbuck, I am old. Shake hands with me,

man." Ahab held his hand up from his boat.

Their hands met. Starbuck had tears in his eyes.

"Oh, my captain, my captain!—don't go—don't go! I am a brave man, but I cry when I think of what thou art about to do."

"Lower me away!" cried Ahab, tossing Starbuck's arm from him. "Stand by the crew! Man the boats!"

Not even the good sense of loyal Starbuck could change Ahab's mind. Sharks surrounded Ahab's boat, snapping and tearing at its oars. Starbuck shuddered as he watched Ahab's boat pull away. He thought about his wife and little boy, and his home he might never see again. As he looked upward to the heavens, a hawk tore the red flag from the ship's mast and flew away.

The boats had not gone far when Ahab realized that Moby Dick lay somewhere deep below. He stopped and held his boat against the waves directly over the spot where the whale had disappeared when it dove.

"Ha! Strike, ye waves!" he cried. "But ye strike a thing with no cover! There can be no coffin without a lid. There will be no hearse for me. And only a rope can kill me! Ha! Ha!"

Suddenly the waters around him swelled in wide circles, then rose up as if an iceberg were pushing from below. There was a low, rumbling sound—a deep hum. Everyone held his breath as a huge hulk, dragging ropes, harpoons, and spears behind it, shot from the sea. Then it crashed back into the deep, exploding the water into a shower thirty feet high.

"Now!" cried Ahab, and the boats darted forward to attack. Yesterday's harpoons were still sticking in him. As if in a mad rage, Moby Dick charged. His flapping tail and horrible white forehead threw the boats aside. All the harpoons from the boats of the two mates were lost overboard and the bows of both boats were torn apart. Somehow, Ahab's boat was not damaged.

While Daggoo and Tashtego were trying to fix their leaking boats, the whale turned and shot by them again. At that moment, a terrible cry went up.

Lashed to the whale's back was Fedallah's body! He was pinned tightly by the harpoon lines which the monster's rolling had wrapped around him. His braided hair was in wild shreds, and his bulging eyes were staring straight at old Ahab.

The harpoon dropped from Ahab's hand.

"Tricked! Fooled! Aye, Fedallah, I see thee again! And I see that thou goest before me and that this is the hearse not made by human hands that thou didst promise. But I hold thee to the last letter of thy word. Where is the second hearse? Away mates! Your boats are no good now. Go back to the ship and repair them if ye can. But my own men—Down! I'll harpoon the first man to jump from this boat! Ye are my arms and legs, and so obey me. Where's the whale?"

He turned and saw Moby Dick swimming past the *Pequod* in a direction that would take him away from them and out to sea. Ahab headed his boat toward the whale.

"Oh, Ahab!" cried Starbuck from the ship. "It is not too late, even now on the third day, not too late to stop the mad chase. See! Moby Dick is not seeking thee. It is thou, thou, that is madly seeking him!"

As Ahab's boat passed nearby the ship, he could see Starbuck's face at the rail. Waving to him, Ahab told him to turn the ship and follow the whale. Looking up he could see the brave harpooners, Queequeg, Tashtego, and Daggoo, climbing the three masts. Carpenters were at work repairing the damaged boats. He could see

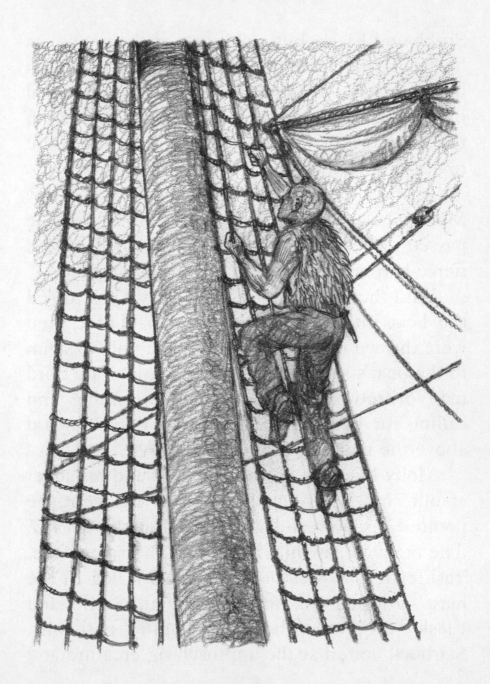

Stubb and Flask, busy making new harpoons. As he heard the hammers working on the broken boats, another hammer seemed to drive a nail into his heart. He saw that the flag was gone from the mast and he shouted to Tashtego to be sure to get another flag and nail it to the top.

Ahab looked back toward the water and saw Moby Dick charging straight at him. When he passed close enough, Ahab stood and flung his fierce harpoon and cursed the hated whale.

With the sting of the steel, Moby Dick tossed the boat into the air with his tail. Three men were thrown into the sea. Two were able to swim to the boat's side and struggle back in. The third man drifted away in the sea, swimming and calling for help. His voice could not be heard above the roar of the waves.

Moby Dick now turned himself and his anger at our ship. Picking up speed as he went, he pointed his powerful white head at the *Pequod*. The crew all saw him coming at the same time. Tashtego, who was nailing the new flag to the mast, stopped his arm in mid-air. Stubb and Flask dropped their half-built harpoons. Starbuck stared at the approaching creature and

began to pray. Queequeg, Daggoo, and the rest of the crew did not move. Their eyes were locked on the giant beast rushing toward the ship. With a sickening crunch, a hundred tons of muscle, bone and white anger crashed into the ship. Men and masts shook and fell as the sea waters rushed like a river through the hole in the ship's side.

"The ship! The hearse! The second hearse!" cried Ahab from the boat. "Its wood could only be American!"

Ahab turned from the sinking, dying ship to see Moby Dick lying still in the water. Coming nearer to the whale, Ahab picked up the last harpoon and shouted out a string of oaths and curses full of hate.

"For evil's sake I stab at thee! For hate's sake I spit my last breath at thee. Let all coffins and hearses sink into the same pool! Now I give thee my final spear!"

The harpoon struck. The injured whale flew forward, pulling the harpoon line with it at lightning speed. The line looped and twisted. Ahab bent to clear the line, and when he did, it caught and tightened like a noose around his neck. Without a sound, Ahab shot out of the boat.

Before the crew even knew he was gone, he had disappeared into the ocean—killed by his own rope. Fedallah's dark promise had come true.

For an instant, the poor crew in Ahab's boat looked in shock, then turned. "The ship! Great God, where is the ship?" Their eyes filled with terror when they saw only the top parts of the masts still above water. There on the masts hung the harpooners, still keeping their lookouts on the sea. Now, a great whirlpool formed as the ship slipped further down into the water. The force of the whirlpool's pull caught the small boat. With one last rushing sound, the crew, every oar, every harpoon, and every last splinter of the *Pequod* were drawn to the center of the black hole and carried out of sight.

Small birds flew crying over the whirlpool. Slowly, the sides of the dark watery hole slid to its center; then all collapsed. The water became still and calm. The great shroud of the sea rolled on as it rolled five thousand years ago.

CHAPTER THIRTY-TWO

The Rest of the Story

And I only am escaped alone to tell thee. —Job

The story is over. The action is done. Why then is someone speaking?—Because one did survive the wreck.

It so happened that after Fedallah's disappearance, I was the one picked to take his place in Ahab's boat. I was among those three seamen who, on that last day, were tossed from the rocking boat, and I was the one who floated away, given up for lost.

As I watched with horror from a distance, the whirlpool's edge began to pull me slowly to its center. By the time I neared that point, the water had begun to calm down and was just a creamy pool, turning slowly around. I floated in lazy circles around the dark hole until, all at once, up from the center shot the coffin life buoy built by my friend, Queequeg. It landed near me and floated by my side.

I was held above water by that coffin for almost one whole day and night, floating on a calm, peaceful sea. Even the circling sharks glided by as if their jaws were locked shut. The savage sea vultures sailed with closed beaks. On the second day, a sail drew near, and I was picked up at last.

It was the sad *Rachel*. In her search for her missing children she found only me, Ishmael.

THE END

HERMAN MELVILLE

Herman Melville was born on August 1, 1819, in New York City, the third child in a family of eight children. When Herman was only twelve years old, his father died, leaving the family with little money.

Herman worked at a variety of jobs to help support himself and his family. He got his first taste of the sea in 1839 when he sailed on a merchant ship to Liverpool, England, and back. Two years later, he signed on the whale ship *Acushnet*, which took him throughout the Pacific over the next three years.

By 1844, Melville had seen enough of harsh sea life and settled down to write about his adventures. He was married in 1847 to Elizabeth Shaw, a childhood friend. His first sea story, *Typee*, was published two years later. He completed *Moby Dick* in 1851.

Melville authored scores of books and articles. His last novel, *Billy Budd*, was completed just months before his death on September 28, 1891. Over the years, Melville has come to be regarded as one of America's great writers, and *Moby Dick* his greatest achievement.